Playing With Dolls

Jesse enjoys playing with dolls and wearing girls' clothing and everyone from his parents, teachers, friends and neighbors assumes he will grow up gay. As an adult the burden of those assumptions hampers his ability to come to terms with his sexuality"

Korin I. Dushayl "has done a great job depicting a young man's journey in discovering his true self."
Allena Gabosch, Executive Director
Center for Sex Positive Culture

"How one is labeled versus how one experientially comes to self-identification held a captivating tension for me. ... the everyday details in the story created a realistically immersive landscape that made it easier to viscerally identify with the characters."
Mark Silver

Korin I. Dushayl "has accomplished something remarkable here, crafting a story that works on all levels — educating, arousing, inspiring, empowering, and (most importantly) emotionally connecting with the reader."
Sally Bibrary, Bending the Bookshelf

As a FemDom, I.G. Frederick knows first hand the beauty of symbiotic D/s relationships filled with love. As an observer she sees the many ways BDSM turns ugly. She writes about abusive and tragic interactions as Korin I. Dushayl.

I.G. Frederick trades words for cash, specializing in erotic and transgressive fiction and poetry since 2001. Her erotic short stories appeared in Hustler Fantasies,

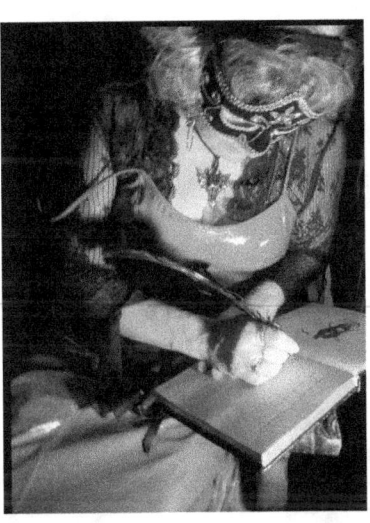

Forum, Foreplay, and Desire Presents, as well as electronic, audio, and print anthologies. Her novels receive high praise from readers, critics, and other authors.

Ms. Frederick, owns the man she adores who although dominant in the rest of his life, demonstrates his love by serving as her submissive.

http://transgressivewriter.com

Playing With Dolls

"A must read for anyone who ever had to learn how to be comfortable in their own skin."

"A sensitive and believable account of a young man's struggle to both sexual and social self-realization."

Sharazade
erotica writer, editor,
reviewer, publisher

Korin I. Dushayl
Author of *Broken* and *Shattered*

Playing With Dolls
First Edition
© **2012 by I.G. Frederick**

ISBN: 978-1-937471-98-9

Pussy Cat Press
http://pussycatpress.com/publisher.html/
P.O. Box 19764
Portland OR 97280

Dedication

To Robin and all my other misunderstood,
transgender friends who suffer
society's prejudice and abuse.

Chapter One

Jesse Andrews twisted one strand of his sandy brown hair around and around his finger, trying not to look at his mother who wept, her shoulders shaking. Their counseling sessions always ended the same way: his mother crying, his dad holding her, the counselor sitting behind her wood-topped metal desk, hands tented above her blotter, lips pursed in disapproval.

"I'm afraid that's all the time we have today, folks. We can continue where we left off next week."

Releasing his hair, Jesse picked invisible lint from his blouse. "My birthday's next week."

The counselor rifled through her thick folder of notes. "Your birthday's on Friday, our appointment's on Thursday."

Smoothing his skirt over his thighs, Jesse steeled himself before looking up at the counselor. She wore thick, black-framed glasses and kept her black hair cut shorter than his dad's.

"I'll be eighteen. I should get to decide if I want to continue counseling."

Her eyes widened. His mother gasped, and his dad cleared his throat.

"Jesse, do you really think the need to resolve your communications problems with your family ends when you turn eighteen? You still have another year at South Eugene and you'll continue living with your parents while you attend U of O."

"We've come here every week for the last two years and nothing's changed. I'd have graduated by now if they hadn't decided I couldn't start school until I was a year older than everyone else." Jesse crossed one leg over the other, pulling the skirt taut.

"Son, we just didn't want you getting beat up all the time for being different." His dad touched Jesse's arm. "We thought if you had a year's growth on everyone else ..."

The only thing he'd ever heard the counselor say that made any sense was that his dad constantly called him "son" because he needed to remind himself that he'd fathered a boy. That revelation, however, hadn't changed his dad's habit of using the word until Jesse cringed.

"Whatever. I think we've wasted enough time and money. We never get past that Dad accepts I'm gay, but Mother can't cope with the fact that I'll never get married and have kids. I don't want to keep blowing an hour and a half I could spend studying and lord knows how much money that could go to tuition."

His dad threw up his hands and scowled. "Son..."

Jesse turned and glared at him, which stopped his words although not his frown.

His mother pulled more tissues from the ever-present box on the desk.

The counselor pressed her index finger against the manila cover of the folder and leaned forward. "Young man, do you really think you're qualified to determine whether or not your family needs or benefits from counseling?"

"Don't need qualifications to see that nothing's improved since the school made us come see you." Jesse stood up, clutching his purse, and gave his dad a pleading look.

His dad pulled his mother to her feet, cradling her against his chest. Her tears wet his blue jersey knit shirt. "Umm, why don't you cancel next week, Lorraine. I'll call you if we want to set up additional appointments after that."

"I can't keep the time slot open if you're not willing to commit." The counselor flipped the page in her calendar and erased their names from the following week's schedule. Jesse could only see one other appointment that day.

"I understand. Thanks for everything. We'll be in touch." His dad kept one arm around his mother and reached for the door with the other. Jesse followed them out to the blue Prius parked at the curb.

Chapter Two

Jesse stood in front of the mirror, turning from side to side, admiring the way his new pink satin skirt swirled around his legs. David, who he'd dated for almost six months, had promised him a special surprise for his birthday and Jesse wanted to look his best. He reached under the skirt trying to pull the edge of his black chiffon blouse taut, then changed his mind, dragged it out, and draped it over the skirt waistband. He frowned and tucked it in again. It didn't fit right without any padding on top, but he'd never liked falsies.

David's plans probably included sex. Although the idea didn't excite Jesse, he'd always felt left out when the other boys hanging out at Skinner Butte got together to brag. David had stuck around longer than anyone else, despite Jesse's refusal to go beyond kissing and petting. Flattered by the attention of an older man, a college sophomore, Jesse decided he'd let David have his way tonight. He didn't want to start adulthood still a virgin.

When he came down the stairs, David already sat in the living room chatting up Jesse's parents. They seemed to get along better with David than previous, younger dates.

"Aren't you just gorgeous," Dad said.

His mother just sat in the easy chair wearing the tight smile that never included her eyes.

Jesse smiled at David who sat on the sofa, his arms folded across his chest. Although he claimed to envy Jesse his parents' acceptance, David still didn't like picking Jesse up for dates. "Your parents're just too weird for me," David had said more than once. "Most of the guys I date pretend we're just going out together to pick up girls." Despite his mother's attitude, Jesse had no wish to leave the house dressed in jeans with his drag in a backpack so he could change in a bathroom somewhere.

David stood. "You ready? We should get going."

Jesse gave David a peck on the cheek, careful not to smudge his lipstick or leave any on David's skin.

"You have a fun birthday celebration, son." Dad draped an arm over Jesse's shoulders.

Jesse avoided cringing, but ducked under his father's embrace to take David's hand. "Ready when you are."

David pulled him out into the bright sun and warmth of summer. "Are you really, ready?"

Jesse swallowed and nodded. Part of him was, anyway.

David treated him to his favorite restaurant, the Pearl Street Ice Cream Parlour. After burgers and fries, they shared the "For Me and My Gal" concoction -- cake with two kinds of ice cream and sauces. Although they battled with spoons for the best bits, David let Jesse have the cherry and kept his promise not to tell anyone it was Jesse's birthday. When the drum came out announcing two other celebrants, they joined other patrons in singing "Happy Birthday." With a mischievous glint in his brown eyes, David mouthed Jesse's name instead of the one shouted out by the restaurant crew.

When they walked out of the restaurant, one of the boys from Jesse's algebra class stomped up the steps leading a couple of girls Jesse recognized and a guy he'd never seen before. "Jess?" Bethany asked.

Jesse flinched. "It's Jesse." He sighed. "Not Jess."

Jim, South Eugene's starting quarterback, flicked up the hem of Jesse's skirt. "Honey, if you're going to dress like this, we should call you Jessica."

"Oh, leave him alone." Bethany pushed at Jim, trying to get him to enter the restaurant. "You promised us a Volcano."

"Him? Don't you mean her?" Jim pinched Jesse's cheek. "You could give the girls lessons on how to dress for a date. Look at them, both wearing jeans."

Bethany's jeans looked painted on and Lori's had studs across her ass. Jesse thought they both looked prettier than he did. He admired their narrow waists, curvaceous hips, and the pert mounds that made their cheap tee shirts look far sexier than his more costly blouse.

Lori took Jim's hand. "Why do you always harass the poor boy? He's not bothering you. Now, if he was prettier than me, I might worry." She shook her long blond hair back from her shoulders and batted mascara-darkened eye lashes over baby blue eyes.

Jim let her pull him into the restaurant. Jesse gave

Bethany a grateful smile. "See you when school starts, Jesse." She winked.

"Come on, sweetie." David took Jesse's hand and pulled him toward his scooter. It irked Jesse that David hadn't challenged Jim, but the boy did outweigh David by at least fifty pounds. Jesse refrained from complaining, put on his helmet, and climbed on behind David. He put one hand on either side of the older man's waist and David set off for U of O. He didn't turn in, just continued up Eleventh until it merged into Franklin. Jesse wondered what else David had planned besides sex, but just past the campus, David turned into the Days Inn parking lot.

Chapter Three

David didn't stop at the lobby. He drove around to the back and pulled into a parking spot near the end. After they dismounted, David led Jesse through a doorway, up a flight of stairs, and halfway down the hall. He fished a card key out of his shirt pocket. When the green light came on, he opened the door, stood aside and gestured Jesse into the room.

"I thought this'd be nicer for your first time than a dorm room with my roommate banging on the door. No one'll interrupt us here." David flashed the "Do Not Disturb" sign at Jesse before he hung it on the outside handle. He closed the door and the click of the lock made Jesse gasp.

He tried to calm himself by looking around. A green and yellow quilted bedspread covered the king sized bed and a picture of a heron flying over a marsh hung above the oak-trimmed white headboard. A box of condoms and a large bottle of lube sat on one white melamine-covered bedside table. The sight made him gulp. His dad made him promise never to have sex without a condom. At least three of the guys he'd dated lost interest when he let them know he required latex.

In front of the curtained window, a small square table sat flanked by two ladder-backed chairs and a stuffed armchair filled the corner.

David sat in the armchair. "Come here, my pretty." He held out his hands.

Jesse hesitated until he saw David's brows pull together, then stepped forward and let him take one hand in each of his. He kissed the back of each one in turn before pulling Jesse closer, guiding him onto his lap. David put one hand behind his neck and kissed him. Jesse closed his eyes and tried to get lost in the moment. But he tasted peppermint and remembered the candy that had come with the check. He didn't feel anything like the excitement described by his friends or that he'd seen in movies.

David caressed his lips with his tongue, urging him to open his mouth. Maybe he shouldn't give his virginity to this man, Jesse thought. Maybe he should wait for someone special. David kept his mouth clamped on his while unbuttoning his blouse. His breathing got heavier, but Jesse's remained normal. Against his ass, he could feel David getting hard even through his jeans. He had no such reaction.

David pushed his blouse off his shoulders and his mouth moved down Jesse's neck. He thought about leaving, but David had already paid for the room. He expected him to be on the receiving end, so if Jesse didn't get hard, it wouldn't matter. He sighed. David chuckled and fumbled with the button at the waist of his skirt. Perhaps if he tried another tact, Jesse could get it up before David discovered his lack of enthusiasm.

Jesse slid off David's lap and knelt between his legs. Pulling the leather through the buckle, he undid David's belt and unbuttoned his jeans. The man's erection poked through his briefs. David pulled Jesse's head toward his cock.

He would have liked more time to contemplate the beauty he'd read so much about, but Jesse also wanted to move things along. He stuck out his tongue and licked the shaft. Tolerable. It tasted a little of Irish Spring. Encouraged, he slipped his lips around the glans. David gasped. Jesse took a deep breath through his nostrils and tried to slide his lips down the shaft. David pushed his hips upward into Jesse's face. He gagged and pulled away, choking.

"It's okay." David sat forward to kiss his forehead and stroke his hair. "You need to take it slow until you get used to taking something this big."

Jesse scrunched up his face. David didn't seem as long as he did when he got hard. He swallowed and tried again.

David kept one hand lightly on the back of his head, but didn't push against it. "Breathe through your nose." His cock twitched in Jesse's mouth. He grimaced, but he managed to slide his lips halfway down the shaft and back up again.

"Oh, yeah," David sighed and thrust upward.

Jesse sucked, hoping that would work as well and wouldn't involve having a cock shoved down his throat.

"Yeah, baby."

Encouraged, Jesse sucked on the glans and lashed at it with his tongue.

David's hips bucked, but he didn't force himself further into Jesse's mouth. "Damn, I've waited so long for this. It feels so fucking good."

Jesse dutifully sucked and licked until David grabbed his head with one hand on either side and pushed Jesse's head up and down on his cock. "Shit, I'm gonna spurt. Swallow it? For me, please."

Jesse's stomach roiled as hot, salty jizz filled his mouth, but he managed to choke it down without tossing up his dinner. He sat back on his heels.

David leaned against the back of the chair with his eyes closed, a satisfied smile on his face. "Definitely worth waiting for." He stood up and stripped off his jeans and underwear, tossing them on the chair, then he reached for Jesse's skirt.

Jesse lifted his hands to get them out of David's way and somehow they ended up on the other man's shoulders. Once the skirt and Jesse's panties fell to the floor, David pulled Jesse to him, pressing their bodies together. David had gotten hard again, Jesse still hung limp.

"Don't be frightened, baby." David reached between them and ran one finger along Jesse's cock. "I promise I'll make it good for you. I want your first time to be something special, something you'll always remember."

Jesse sighed with relief as David's stroking finally raised the dead. He stripped everything else from his senses and concentrated on the one finger running up and down until he got respectably hard. David grabbed him and squeezed. Jesse gasped. His breathing got ragged. Still gripping his cock, David pulled Jesse's face to his with his other hand. He pressed their lips together and shoved his tongue into Jesse's mouth.

He went limp again, but fortunately David released him before noticing. Turning Jesse around so he faced the bed, David nudged Jesse's shoulders until he got the hint. He lay face down on the bed, his rear in the air. He heard lube splurting out and then felt a cold finger massaging his ass. He clenched up, bile rising to his throat.

"Relax, baby. I don't want to hurt you." David ran his finger around and around Jesse's asshole.

Jesse swallowed and managed to relax enough so his ass cheeks unclenched. David pushed his finger in a little ways and turned it back and forth. Jesse wanted to cry. David reached between his legs with his other hand and caressed his balls while he pressed his finger deeper into Jesse's ass. He tried to keep his breathing even, tried not to clench up, to relax. He just wanted to get it over with.

David had two fingers up his ass, now, dragging them in and out. "Damn, you're so tight."

Jesse bit his lip and waited. At least it didn't really hurt. When he heard the condom package rip open, part of him wanted to grab his clothes and run from the room. But he couldn't face the embarrassment of explaining why to David. Hell, he couldn't explain his urge to run away to himself. For the past two years, he'd assessed the potential of every male he dated, trying to decide who he wanted to pop his cherry. Now he'd finally found someone who cared enough to wait until he was ready, someone who didn't give him grief about insisting on condoms, who forked over money for a hotel room so they could have some privacy. And, now he couldn't even keep it up.

David still had his lubed finger inside him. "This is going to feel so good," he whispered in a hoarse voice. He worked in another finger.

Jesse grimaced, grateful David couldn't see his face.

"Relax, baby." David's baritone soothed his ear and reminded him how much the older man cared for him.

Jesse took deep breaths and tried to ease the tension from his shoulders. It really didn't matter if he stayed hard or even if he came. More than anything, he needed to not be an eighteen-year-old virgin.

Panting, David eased the head of his cock in and Jesse felt an overwhelming urge to poop. His face grew hot as the sensation grew and he wondered if he should confess and run to the bathroom. The last thing he wanted to do was to shit all over his lover.

"Bear down, like you're taking a dump." David had one hand on Jesse's ass and the other on his waist, urging him to open up.

He tried to comply and David slowly pushed himself all the way in. It really wasn't too bad. Jesse let out the breath he hadn't realized he'd been holding. David pulled back then pushed into Jesse again. It was only a little uncomfortable and Jesse found he could set that aside. He distracted himself by counting the repeating pattern in the bedspread, while David slid slowly in and out of his ass. It took David longer to come the second time and Jesse wondered which would be worse for long periods of time: having his ass fucked or sucking cock.

He could hear David's breathing accelerate, feel his

heart beating rapidly against his back, and the man's sweat dripping onto his skin. David's pace increased until he shouted out and pushed deep inside. He lay panting, resting his chest against Jesse's back before easing out of his ass and flopping onto the bed. He pulled Jesse into his arms. "You okay, lover?"

Jesse nodded, his head moving up and down against David's chest. He resisted when David put one hand under his chin and tried to turn his face upward, wrapping his arms around the other mans's chest, hiding his face in the bristly hairs. David stroked his head, and all he could think about was whether those were the fingers that had been inside his ass.

David kissed him and Jesse wondered what he expected next. He really just wanted to go home and take a shower. But David had released his mouth and was kissing his way down Jesse's chest. Jesse groaned. He couldn't think of anything more mortifying than not getting an erection while David sucked his cock. Desperately, he closed his eyes and concentrated on the image he used when he masturbated, the one that had always done the trick, ever since he found it in a stack of porn in his cousin's bedroom.

That, combined with the soft kisses on his cock, got Jesse hard. His breath came in short, sharp gasps, and he could feel the tension building in his balls. Afraid if he included David in his fantasy, he'd lose his erection again, Jesse kept his hands by his side and his mind as far away from the man sucking him as he could manage. When he finally shot his load into David's mouth, he almost cried in relief.

"That was wonderful." He lied. Although he'd enjoyed

the sensations, he could get the same results with his hand without having to endure the rest.

David lifted his head, grinning and licking cream off his lips. "Happy Birthday, baby."

Jesse wanted to puke. David stretched out beside him and pulled him into his arms. Not knowing what else to do, Jesse let David's shoulder cradle his head, grateful the man didn't try to kiss him again. He relaxed while David stroked his back, enjoying the cuddling, and snuggled closer. He wrapped one arm around David's waist, content to lay beside him in silence.

"I knew you'd be more comfortable if we had some privacy for your first time." David played with Jesse's hair. "But, I can't afford to do this every week. I'm afraid you'll have to get used to taking our turn in the dorm room."

Jesse pressed his lips together. He wasn't sure he could ever endure this again, especially if he had to worry about David's roomie walking in on them with his girlfriend. "Thanks for making it special," he whispered.

Chapter Four

When David finally dropped Jesse off at home, he beat a hasty retreat to the bathroom. In the shower, he scrubbed his skin with a washcloth and shampooed his hair twice. When he got out, he brushed his teeth and filled his mouth with mouthwash.

He'd hoped to slink off to bed, but his dad waited for him when he opened the bathroom door. "Normally, one spends an hour in the bathroom before a date, not after."

Jesse crumpled. He threw himself against his dad's broad chest, burying his nose in his shoulder, and sobbed. At first his dad stood there, but then he wrapped Jesse in his big strong arms, patting his back and rubbing his head.

"What's wrong, son? Did that boy hurt you?"

Jesse shook his head without lifting his cheek from the tee shirt, damp with his own tears. He had no idea how to explain his grief to his dad. He didn't know if he should have waited for someone else or if that would have made any difference. At Skinner Butte, the guys all raved about how great it was no matter who they fucked. Maybe Jesse just didn't like sex.

"C'mon, let's get out of the hall." His dad wrapped one arm across Jesse's back and guided him toward his room. "Don't want to upset your mother." They sat on the twin bed with the My Little Pony bedspread and Jesse appreciated his dad's silent acceptance. He knew he could talk to his dad, once he figured out what to say. For now, he just needed comfort. Dad was good at that. Jesse didn't have to worry about upsetting his dad or what the tight smile might mean this time.

After twenty minutes, when still hadn't spoken, his dad stood up. "You'd better get to sleep, son. Don't you have to be at work early tomorrow?"

"Thanks, Dad." Jesse wiped the back of his hand under his eyes.

"You know I'm always available to discuss whatever's troubling you?"

Jesse managed a smile.

"That's better. Get some sleep." His dad left the room, closing the door behind himself. Jesse crawled into bed.

Jesse ignored David's calls and text messages and stayed away from Skinner Butte. In addition to his summer job at PC Market, he took two summer school classes, and signed on to volunteer with Basic Rights Oregon to fight against the measure that would make gay marriage unconstitutional in Oregon. He could vote for the first time in the fall election, and he wanted to support gay rights. But the only presidential candidate he could really get excited about had dropped out last February.

He spent lots of time on Friendster and MySpace arguing against the measure's discriminatory language. It beat arguing with his mother who was always complaining that John Kerry supported civil unions but was against same-sex marriage. Jesse never understood why she considered marriage so important. He'd no desire to get married, ever. He didn't even want to date anymore.

Still, when Marc, the cutest guy at the Market, asked him out, Jesse couldn't say no. If he dated someone else, maybe David'd stop calling. And, he reassured himself, he could always quit seeing Marc before things got sexual. Or not. Maybe he'd enjoy sex with Marc. But, Marc didn't ring Jesse's chimes, either.

Chapter Five

"**I**'ve talked to a couple of women from my AAUW Chapter about having you come do a presentation about Measure 36." His mother kept pushing him to speak about the impact Measure 36 would have on his future to her friends.

"Thanks, Mom. I'm not that great a speaker." Jesse sat on the stool next to his mother's easel watching her paint. He reminded himself she wasn't trying to put him on the spot. She just wanted to help. "But I know several couples available to speak to any groups that'll listen. One of them's been together for almost twenty years."

He tried to figure out what she was painting, but all he saw was a swirl of colors on the canvas. His mother always gave her paintings names that made him think he was missing something. "If you let me know the dates, I can make all the arrangements for you."

His mother shrugged. "I'll have Stacy give you a call and you two can take care of the details." She didn't want someone to speak to her group, he realized. She wanted him to. After staring at the canvas for several minutes, she added a dot of blue. "Are we taking door hangers around again this weekend?"

Jesse had volunteered to canvas households in Creswell, about thirteen miles south of Eugene, but he dared not take his mother. She turned ferocious when confronting anti-gay rhetoric. With more than sixty percent of Creswell expected to vote for Bush again, Jesse knew he'd meet a lot of resistance. "I've got other plans Saturday, but we can go Sunday if you want."

His mother smiled. For the first time since he remembered, they had something in common. Even though they had dissimilar approaches, and completely different reasons for opposing the measure, the campaign *had* drawn them closer together.

Sunday they headed east to Springfield with his mother at the wheel of the Prius. Jesse wore jeans and a tee shirt that had a red circle with a slash through the words "Measure 36."

"Have you thought about what you're going to major in at U.O. next fall?" Jesse's mother usually wanted to talk about the amendment and her hopes he could get married someday. Jesse's jaw clenched at this new topic.

"Don't have to declare a major for two years, not until my sophomore year. Figured I'd start with liberal arts courses and general requirements." Jesse knew exactly what he wanted to study. What he didn't know was how to tell his mother.

"Don't they have aptitude tests to help you figure out your best career options?" She parked on residential street a few blocks south of Highway 126.

Jesse retrieved a bundle of door hangers from the

back seat and handed them to her. They also bore the circle crossing out Measure 36 on one side and bullet points explaining the civil rights issues at stake on the other. He took another bundle and stepped out of the car.

"We'll talk more on the way back." His mother smiled and started toward the front door of the nearest house. "Maybe we'll stop for ice cream."

Crossing the street to work the other side, Jesse wondered how he could avoid that conversation. Walking from house to house, hanging bright cardboard from door knobs, he put the coming confrontation out of his mind.

He only had a few hangers left when he rounded a corner and saw half a dozen teenagers lounging on a front porch. They wore olive fatigue pants held up by suspenders, wife beater tops, and Doc Martens boots. The white frame house had a weed-infested lawn and two partially assembled automobiles in the driveway. The boys all had buzz cuts and Jesse could see most of them had black tattoos on their biceps.

Jesse turned on his heel, but one of the shouted. "Where you goin', faggot?"

"You lost, pervert?" Another voice chimed in. "You should know better than to leave Fairyland. We don't want your kind over on this side."

Jesse didn't have to look back. He heard their boots marching on the sidewalk behind him. He ran. The pounding of boots on pavement got faster. He dashed across the street and spotted a car approaching the stop sign. Jesse ran straight to it and yanked the passenger door open.

"Please, help me. They're chasing me." Without waiting for the driver's response, he got in, slammed the door, and pushed the lock closed.

One of the Skinheads tried to open the door. He beat on the glass when he couldn't. The driver, a middle-aged man wearing a blue polo shirt and white slacks looked from Jesse to the gang surrounding the car and back. "What the hell do you think you're doing in my car. Get out. Now."

Jesse stared at the man. "Please, sir, just give me a ride for a few blocks. If you make me get out here, they'll beat me up."

"Hmpf. You probably deserve it. What the hell're you doing over here, anyway?" He pointed to the hangers in Jesse's hand. "We don't need your faggot propaganda. God intended marriage to be one man and one woman. Homos are an abomination."

The Skinheads pounded their fists on the car windows and Jesse feared they would break one. Fortunately, the driver pulled away from the stop sign and drove several blocks until the Skinheads stopped running after the car. As soon as they gave up their chase, the man turned the corner and screeched to a halt.

"Get out of my car, you little pervert, or I'll call the police." He extracted a cell phone from his shirt pocket.

Jesse fumbled with the lock until he got the car door open. He got out then realized he'd probably be better off if the driver did call the police. Afraid the Skinheads could find him if he stopped to call now, he ran down the block hoping he was heading in the right direction. Heart racing, gasping for breath, Jesse ran through the neighborhood and took so many turns that he soon had no idea where he was in relationship to the highway. He stopped with his hands on his thighs, trying to catch his breath, listening for the sound of boots on pavement.

He could hear a lawn mower in the distance and the strains of country music coming from a nearby house. Crows cawed and a wind chime tinkled in the slight breeze. No boots. Jesse walked to the corner so he could see the street sign and debated whether he should call the cops or his mother. Still panting, he took out his cell phone and pushed six.

"Where are you, Jesse? I put up the entire bundle of hangers and started on another."

Jesse took a deep breath. "I got kind of confused and I'm not sure where I am. Do you think you could come get me?"

"Why in the world can't you just come back to the car?"

"I'm at Fifteenth and Bell." Jesse walked away from the corner up the nearest driveway. He felt too exposed on the street and he'd no idea how long it would take him to persuade his mother to come rescue him. He should have called the cops.

"I've no idea where that is, dear. I'm at Tenth and Quinalt. Can't you just find your way back to the car? I'll keep putting up hangers until you do."

"I really don't feel well." Jesse crouched down behind the mini-van parked in front of the garage. His stomach churned and he just wanted to go home and hide, curled up under the covers of his bed.

"Why didn't you say so, dear? I'll be there as soon as I figure out where you are."

Jesse closed his phone and burst into tears. When he

saw his mother's blue Toyota pull up to the corner a few minutes later, he wiped his face on the hem of his tee shirt and walked out to the car.

"Goodness, what's wrong with you, Jesse?" His mother stared at him. "Have you been crying?"

"Please, Mom, can we just go home now. I really don't feel good."

"Should I take you to Urgent Care?" Thankfully his mother put the car in gear and headed back to the highway.

Jesse pulled his seat belt around his chest and buckled it. "No, I probably just got dehydrated because of the heat. I'll be okay with some water and a nap." He reached into the back seat to retrieve his bottle. The water tasted warm and insipid, but he didn't care. He could still feel his pulse pounding in his ears.

When they reached their own driveway, Jesse jumped out of the car before his mother shut off the engine. He ran into the house and up the stairs to the safety of his room where he stripped out of his clothing and climbed into bed with Jeremiah. With the sheet over his head and the worn, stuffed bear clutched to his chest, he finally calmed down enough for his heartbeat to slow and his breathing to return to normal.

He wanted to tell someone what had happened, but he didn't know who. The tears started again, and Jesse stifled his sobs so his mother wouldn't hear them. Tomorrow he'd report the incident to the coordinator at the BRO office. He hoped Sylvia would come up with office work for him. He didn't think he could go out canvassing or putting up door hangers again.

Chapter Six

Sylvia tried to persuade Jesse to file a police report. He just wanted to forget about it, and couldn't even remember where it all happened.

"You poor thing. You must've been terrified." Sylvia, sitting at the one desk in the office, held her arms open. "Come here, I bet you could use a hug."

Jesse tried to smile, but his lower lip trembled. He could use a hug, but he knew if he accepted one he'd burst into tears again. "I'll be okay, thanks. Just, please, can I work in the office from now on?"

"Of course, dear boy." Sylvia smiled and Jesse sighed with relief. "You can start by entering all these names into the database." She pointed to a pile of sign up sheets from various events.

Jesse spent the rest of the campaign doing clerical tasks. He didn't feel he was making as much of a contribution, but he couldn't face going out on the street again. He hated the idea that the constitutional amendment would disenfranchise all his friends and appreciated any opportunity to invest his energy in something meaningful. When his mother asked him about putting up door hangers, he told her he'd gotten promoted to an office staff position and with that school, and work, he wouldn't have time.

One advantage of working at the Lane County BRO headquarters, Jesse discovered, was the opportunity to meet more of what Sylvia called the "troops." She introduced him to Ashleigh and Rachel in his first week as office gofer. Pretty much inseparable, they'd lived together for six months. Ashleigh, petite with long, red hair and green eyes, worked at Hot Topic in Valley River Center. She favored twirly skirts and low-cut blouses. Rachel changed oil at the Pit Stop on Eleventh. Jesse never saw her wear anything except jeans and men's shirts or tees.

Hanging with the two of them proved so much less stressful than the meat market at Skinner Butte. Jesse knew they'd never have any sexual expectations of him, wouldn't expect him to brag about his exploits, and wouldn't require him to listen to any squicky details about their own relationship. He wasn't sure why he should consider lesbian sex squicky. He'd always enjoyed lesbian porn, but most of the other boys seemed to apply the term to anything involving female genitalia.

They watched the election returns together on November second and cried in each others arms when Measure 36 passed by more than fifty-six percent of the vote. They drank cheap wine and railed about the out-of-state money that fueled the anti-gay initiative. Jesse knew Ashleigh and Rachel hoped to get married one day. Some of the fellows he knew had gotten so excited when Multnomah County in Portland offered marriage licenses to same-sex couples. The depressing news that Bush was reelected got them discussing the option of moving to British Columbia to escape. Jesse knew it'd never happen, but it helped alleviate some of their pain to at least consider the possibility.

After school the next day, the three hung out at Gary's coffee shop, killing time until Ashleigh had to head for the mall. "We got some adorable new things in, yesterday." She unlocked her bright yellow, VW bug. "You wanna come try them on? There's a flounce skirt that'd look divine on you -- show off your legs."

Jesse smiled and climbed in the back seat. When it came to dressing him, Ashleigh's attitude reminded him of the way he used to treat the Barbie dolls that he still had packed away in the back of his closet. But, he enjoyed trying on clothing and she had superb fashion sense.

When they got to the store, Ashleigh clocked in while Jesse helped Rachel look through the Franz Ferdinand, Killers, and Modest Mouse tee shirts for one that wouldn't show oil stains. Ashleigh came out of the back room and led Jesse over to the aisle with skirts, corset tops, and dresses.

She handed him one hanger after another until he juggled half a dozen outfits, then led him to the dressing room. With U2 blaring in the background, Jesse stripped off his jeans and tee shirt, leaving only his Converse high-tops and his pink, nylon panties.

First, he tried on a skirt with several layers of tulle that started halfway down his thighs, growing out of a straight pleather band that wrapped too closely around his ass.

"Nice," commented Rachel. She lounged on the bench across the back of the dressing room watching him pirouette in front of the mirror while Fatboy Slim replaced U2.

"Kinda tight." Jesse tried to adjust the pleather down, but in this skirt he couldn't hide the bulge between his legs. It just didn't look right.

"Nope. Ya got a nice ass. And wearing this skirt, no one hitting on you's gonna get any surprises."

Ashleigh opened the dressing room door and added several more hangers to the ones on the hook. "Hey, I like that." She handed him a wide belt with three rows of grommets. "Here, try this too."

Jesse buckled the belt around his waist. Ashleigh undid it, lowered it to his hips, and buckled it several notches looser so it hung at an angle. She stepped back, admiring her handiwork. Rachel seized the opportunity to encircle her waist with her arms. Ashleigh turned and pressed Rachel up against the wall. The two of them made out, ignoring Jesse. He could have tried on another outfit, but he enjoyed watching them together.

Ashleigh had one hand on Rachel's breast, and the other between her legs, rubbing on her jeans. With their mouths locked together, their moans came out muffled. Jesse, reached behind to unzip the skirt. When he looked down, he realized it had gotten tighter. He turned so his friends wouldn't see his erection and reached for a dress with a full skirt. He could feel his cheeks flushing, and wondered what they would think of his reaction.

Although the skirt on the dress only came down a

few inches below his crotch, it billowed out with layers of tulle, disguising his arousal. He turned and saw Rachel shaking. Ashleigh's hand moved furiously back and forth in her crotch, bouncing to the rhythm of Green Day's "American Idiot." Ashleigh dropped Rachel on the bench. "I'll be back, but I'd better make an appearance. Can't spend too much time back here." She winked at Jesse. "Liked the skirt better."

Jesse pressed his lips together and reached for another outfit. When she returned, he turned in front of the mirror, admiring the way a white dress with colorful polka dots clung to his upper body, but flared out just enough above his hips to conceal any evidence of his gender. He would have to get something to fill the green-bordered strapless top. It gaped out from his chest. Thanks to Ashleigh, he now had a padded, strapless bra at home that would do the trick. He'd gotten over his aversion to falsies once she showed him how lovely a little padding made some outfits look.

"Still like the skirt." Ashleigh didn't really look at Jesse. Rachel had dropped to her knees as soon as the door closed. Ashleigh leaned against the wall and flipped her skirt over Rachel's head.

Jesse didn't want to get embarrassed again. He kept his back to the girls and stripped off the dress, replacing his jeans and tee shirt. "I'll put the rest of this stuff back. I really like this dress, will you get it for me?" He looked at the price tag. "With your discount, it should be about $35. I can pay you next Tuesday."

Ashleigh made a noise that Jesse decided to accept as agreement. He slipped out the door with the rest of the clothing draped over his arm. By the time he hung the last one up in its proper place, he no longer needed to cover his jeans.

Chapter Seven

Jesse decided to confide in his dad first. He hoped to enlist his support before confronting his mother with the news that he wouldn't attend the University of Oregon. The two sat on a sofa at the Strand downtown sipping mochas, an indulgence his mother eschewed in favor of plain drip.

He savored the rich coffee and chocolate for a moment before he spoke. "I've decided on my career path."

"That's great, son." His dad beamed and Jesse cringed. "What've you chosen?"

"Cosmetology." Jesse pressed his lips together and watched the expressions play out across his dad's face. Delight changed to dismay, which resolved into the look Jesse had started thinking of as "he's my son and I love him no matter what."

"Do they teach that at U.O.?" His dad took a sip of his coffee, his face wiped clean of any emotional response.

"Unfortunately not." He took a deep breath. "With the classes I took the past two summers, I can graduate in December. I've already been accepted at the College of Beauty. I start at the beginning of the year." Jesse set his cup down on the low table in front of them. "I'm thinking I might get licensed to do hair so I can get a job right away, then do nail coursework part time."

His dad closed his eyes. "I wish you'd said something sooner, son. I can't believe you're graduating in a few weeks. Your mother isn't going to," he cleared his throat and looked at Jesse. "She's going to be upset that you won't be attending the university."

"But, Dad. It'd take me at least four years to earn a college degree. I haven't found anything there at all that I want to spend my life doing. At least with cosmetology I can start working by next summer, *and* I'll enjoy my job."

His dad took a long sip from his cup then set it down next to Jesse's. "Will cutting hair and painting nails make you happy?"

Jesse smiled. "Yes. I've put a lot of thought into this, Dad. I want to do something useful. I want to do something that makes people beautiful. What's wrong with that?"

"As long as you're not doing this 'cause it's a gay thing to do."

Jesse laughed. "No, I really think I'll enjoy it.." Ashleigh let him experiment on her when he first mentioned interest in a hairstyling career. He loved washing and setting her hair and experimenting with different styles. "If I do well, I can earn a decent living."

His dad nodded. "More than anything else, son, I want *you* to be happy. Tell you what, let me break this to your mother. No reason for you to take the brunt of her reaction."

"I'm a major disappointment to her, aren't I?" Jesse grabbed his cup and chugged the rest of his coffee, blinking to fight back the tears. "She thinks I'm a quitter: I quit counseling, I quit canvassing for Measure 36, and now she'll only see that I'm quitting school."

His dad picked up his cup, but set it on one denim-clad leg, running his finger around and around the rim. "Why did you stop canvassing?" He looked at Jesse. He raised the cup to his lips, but put it back down before taking a drink. "You and your mother had some quality time together, for a change, and I thought you'd finally found something you could connect on."

Jesse had to fight to keep his breathing under control, remembering his terror. "I'd rather not talk about it."

His dad raised one eyebrow. "Did someone hurt you?"

"No, but they tried."

"Why the hell didn't you tell someone? We could have filed a police report, taken them to court."

Jesse shook his head.

His dad opened his arms. Jesse hesitated, mindful of the others sipping coffee, surfing the net on their laptops, and talking on their cell phones. But, just the memory of that day had him shaking. He accepted the comfort of his dad's arms.

The door to his room slammed open. "Your father said you're dropping out of high school, not going to college?" His mother had one hand on her hip, the other on the door knob. Her breathing came in short gasps, and her eyes were red and puffy.

"Actually, I've just graduated early from high school and I start classes at beauty college next week." He supposed he shouldn't be surprised his dad had waited three weeks, until after Christmas, to break the news to his mother.

"How could you?" She pulled a handkerchief from the pocket of her denim jumper and dabbed at her eyes. "Without even discussing it? You had a scholarship. You could have made a difference. Set an example. Instead you're just living up to every bad gay stereotype that exists."

"Couldn't find anything to study that interested me enough to put four years of my life into it. I can be out and working at a decent paying job in less than a year." *And have money for my own apartment where you can't just barge in whenever you please.* He pointed to the stack of beauty magazines next to the bed. "It's a subject I enjoy, and a career I believe I'll excel at."

"Spending your life making barely more than minimum wage, dependent on tips?" She blew her nose into the handkerchief and stuffed it back in her pocket. "I was sure with your interest in the election, you could have studied political science, worked for DeFazio or Wyden, maybe run for office yourself one day, championed gay rights."

"You've sure mapped out an interesting career for me." Jesse ran both his hands through his hair, wondering where she got her ideas. "Just because I don't want to study politics, doesn't mean I won't campaign for candidates I care about and issues that're important to me. You've gotta admit, this last election was pretty discouraging and didn't exactly make anyone young and liberal want to get involved or run for office."

"But this election was exactly *why* young people should get more involved in politics." She took a deep breath and Jesse resigned himself to a long lecture. "If more young people had voted, Bush wouldn't have been reelected, Measure 36 would have failed and you could've found a nice boy, settled down, and gotten married."

He wondered if she had any idea how ridiculous her statement sounded, both because it was so not what he wanted, and because he knew how much she would have liked to substitute girl for boy. "Mom, I know you believe that, but sixty-two million idiots voted for Bush. Despite the war, despite the scandals, despite his lies, he got fifty-one percent of the votes. We may live in a liberal oasis, but we're surrounded by intolerant, bigoted people the minute we cross the city line."

"But how many people didn't vote? How many people your age stayed home?" Her face got redder and her voice louder. "What if you'd kept campaigning for Measure 36 and gotten more people to the polls who'd have voted against Bush? What if you'd worked for the Kerry campaign? If you'd gotten more people to vote for him, they'd have voted against Measure 36, too."

"It wouldn't have changed the outcome. Kerry took Oregon, remember?" Jesse stood and walked to the door, trying to encourage his mother to leave his room.

"But more Kerry supporters would have voted against Measure 36." She held her ground.

Jesse sighed and wished he could get her to do the

math. Despite voting blue, significantly more than fifty percent of Oregon ballots supported the one man, one woman constitutional amendment. "Mom, I know it's my fault that Bush won reelection, that Measure 36 passed, that the state doesn't recycle enough, that we have global warming." He grabbed his purse. "But, I'm going to beauty college anyway, and I really don't care to discuss it with you anymore." He stepped around her and walked down to the front room. She still stood at the top of the stairs when he left the house.

Chapter Eight

"Takin u smplc spcl 2 nite." Ashleigh texted Sunday morning after Jesse's first week at the college. "B @ apt @ 8 to dress."

"Shoes?" He sent back.

"Cvrd."

Jesse wondered what Ashleigh had picked out for him this time. Her tastes had gotten more and more bizarre since the election. She only wore black, usually with lots of metal. She now had at least ten earrings in each ear and piercings in her eyebrow, lower lip, and nose. And those were just the ones he could see. Every time she talked about other ones she'd acquired, he changed the subject. Rachel avoided piercings, at least visible ones, but her arms now had tattoos covering them from wrist to shoulder.

When Jesse objected to some of the clothing they picked out for him, they'd buy it and then he'd feel obligated to wear it for them. Although they liked to dress him up and show him off, unlike most females, they accepted him as he was and had no interest in using him sexually. Jesse still dated men occasionally, but he managed to discourage most sexual advances just by insisting on condoms. If that didn't work, he found an excuse to end the relationship.

He arrived at the apartment wearing his gaff under his jeans so he'd have everything tucked away if they'd picked out something tight. He had his collection of various padded bras and boobage in his backpack along with his makeup.

Rachel answered the door. She wore black leather chaps over black jeans, a black wife beater, and a leather vest. Jesse hoped the outfit Ashleigh chose for him would have some color, but he gave up on that when he saw her.

Jesse stared at Ashleigh whose leather corset cinched her waist and pushed her breasts up into creamy mounds. "Wow, you look hot." She wore a leather mini-skirt, decorated with steel grommets, and thigh-high, lace up boots with three-inch heels. "Umm, you both do," he added without taking his eyes off Ashleigh.

"Consider this a belated graduation present, sweets." Ashleigh gave him a hug and he marveled at the rigidity of her corset. How the hell did she breathe? He inhaled the lavender scent she wore which he always enjoyed.

She pointed to the end of the room where a counter, stove, sink, and fridge along one wall made up their kitchen. On the rickety metal table, sat a large box wrapped in shiny black paper tied with a wide, black, satin ribbon.

"You guys are so sweet." Jesse turned to hug Rachel. She smelled only of leather.

"Go ahead! open it." Rachel gave him a perfunctory squeeze.

Jesse untied the bow and turned the box over so he could slice through the tape.

"Oh, just rip it," Rachel insisted.

"Leave him alone." Ashleigh stepped to Jesse's side. "We've got plenty of time."

Jesse removed the paper intact and opened the priority mail box. They must have ordered his gift from eBay. Inside, he found a leather waist cincher and a pair of size twelve platform patent leather boots. "Wow." He didn't know what to say. He couldn't see wearing this stuff, but he knew the girls expected him to. They obviously planned to go somewhere tonight where these things were appropriate. But, he couldn't wear just the cincher.

He looked up. Ashleigh held the hanger of a slinky black mini-dress. "Picked this up at work today, didn't have time to wrap it."

Jesse smiled and reached out to touch the dress. He loved the feel of spandex. He stripped out of his jeans and tee shirt, draping them over the curved metal back of one of the kitchen chairs. Sliding the dress over his head, he enjoyed the touch of the stretchy, silky fabric against his skin. Reaching for his backpack, he asked, "What kind of boobage does this call for?"

"I think you can skip the falsies tonight, hon." Ashleigh held up the waist cincher. "We'll use this to give you all the curvature you need."

Jesse shrugged. She reached around his waist, settled the cincher in place, and had him hold the sides while she zipped it up in front.

"Okay, grab onto the doorway." Ashleigh nudged Jesse over toward the bathroom.

He put one hand on each side of the door jamb.

"Hold on tight and suck in your breath."

Jesse followed her instructions and Ashleigh yanked on the laces and he had a hard time keeping his balance.

He gasped for air. "Geez, I'm not going to be able to breathe."

"Don't worry, you'll get used to it." She yanked the cords even tighter.

By the time she stopped and tied the thongs together, Jesse really did have trouble breathing. He worked on taking shallow breaths and stepped into the bathroom. When he saw his reflection in the full-length mirror on the back of the door, he decided the discomfort was worth it. The cincher drew his waist into a lovely curve, and even pulled his pecs in for a hint of cleavage. He smiled. "I look just lovely. Thanks so very much."

"Hey, we're not done." Ashleigh held the boots in one hand and his makeup bag in the other.

Jesse grabbed the boots, but he found bending over to put them on difficult with the tight cincher. Ashleigh snapped her fingers. Rachel knelt at his feet, helping him into the boots and zipping them up.

"Excellent." Ashleigh handed Jesse his makeup bag. "Do yourself lovely."

When he emerged from the bathroom forty-five minutes later, both girls whistled. He had used Ashleigh's curling iron to make ringlets in his hair. Figuring they would want a Goth look, he'd used his palest foundation and emphasized his grey eyes with thick, black liner and mascara. He'd foregone rouge and used his darkest red lipstick.

"Perfect." Ashleigh blew him an air kiss. "This will be a night to remember. We promise."

They headed for the door and Rachel grabbed a leather duffle sitting next to it on the floor. Jesse looked at her, head tilted to one side.

"You'll find out later," she said. Rachel tossed the duffle in the trunk and climbed into the back seat. Jesse sighed with relief. He couldn't imagine trying to get back there. He could barely breathe sitting up front. He hoped the boots proved comfortable. He didn't imagine he'd sit down much this evening.

Chapter Nine

ashleigh drove them downtown and parked on Pearl Street. Jesse followed the two of them to Devil's Den. The reader board announced "Fetish Night, over 18 only."

The guy collecting the cover charge had half-inch wide, opalescent blue earlets in both lobes, a labret, eyebrow piercing, and a bull ring through his septum. He checked Jesse's ID and smiled. "Save me a dance, Babe."

"Sure." Jesse dragged his eyes away from the man's metal and stuck his license back into his handbag with his lipstick, some cash, and a couple of condoms. He'd carried the same condoms for six months now. Pierced face inked Jesse's inner wrist with a devil stamp, and winked at him. Jesse followed Rachel and Ashleigh into the club and down a dark narrow stairway.

Nelly Furtado's *Promiscuous* blared from the speakers around the room. He could barely see in the dim light. A disco ball spun in the center of the dance floor. Jesse heard a scream from the far left side. No one else seemed to notice. A skinny boy who looked about Jesse's age stood naked except for a thong in a corner section roped off by a metal chain. Four leather cuffs bound his wrists and ankles to a wooden, X-shaped cross. A dark-haired woman, dressed in a leather outfit similar to Ashleigh's, stood behind him with a four-foot whip in her hands, lashing his back. The boy howled again. He already had red welts building up on his shoulders and ass. She kept striking him no matter how loudly he yelled.

Jesse stared, watching the whip leave another nasty red mark on his thighs while the boy cried yet out again. Rachel and Ashleigh moved closer to the chain and stood with their arms around each other's waists, watching. More and more people surged toward the show and Jesse felt alone in a sea of spectators.

The song ended, and the DJ called out. "That boy's in a world of hurt."

"Yeah!" the crowd hollered back.

"We can't let her get away with that, can we?"

"No!" The folks on the dance floor stopped moving. It seemed everyone in the place except Jesse had joined the shouting.

"All together now, let's tell her what we think. Fuck you, bitch!"

"Fuck you, bitch!" everyone yelled in unison.

The woman in the leather corset swung her whip faster and harder, making the boy scream louder.

"Again," shrieked the DJ.

"Fuck you, bitch!"

The woman twirled the whip over her head, repeatedly striking the boy across his shoulders. He sobbed over and over again. Jesse could hear leather slapping skin over the shouting crowd. Although skinny, the boy stood at least a foot taller than the woman wielding the whip. His arms appeared muscular. Jesse couldn't imagine how she could've secured him to the cross if he'd resisted. He wondered what the whip felt like.

The DJ started Justin Timberlake's *Sexyback*. The woman continued to lash the boy with her whip. Every inch of his shoulders, ass, and thighs were covered with red welts. She hung the whip over her shoulder and walked up close to the boy, unclipping his cuffs from the cross. The boy turned and she caught him in her arms. Jesse could see tears glistening in the boy's eyes, but he clung to the woman who'd beaten him. She kissed him on the forehead and he rested his head on her exposed breasts. Someone handed her a chair over the chain and she sat down, bringing the boy to his knees beside her. He laid his head in her lap and she stroked his hair. Jesse found himself longing to trade places with the boy, to have someone stroking his hair while he rested his head like that. He couldn't see that the lashing was much worse than sex, and you still got the cuddling.

Ashleigh leaned over the chain and said something to the woman. She nodded and scooted the chair back away from the cross, taking the boy with her. He wrapped his arms tightly around her waist, keeping his head in her lap. Ashleigh ducked under the chain. Rachel followed, setting her duffle in front of the cross and squatting down on one knee. She unzipped the bag, pulled out a container of cleaning wipes and used one to wipe the surface of the cross. Rachel removed her clothing, folded it neatly, and piled it on a small table next to the cross. Jesse's eyes widened in surprise. Wearing nothing but a black thong, she pulled a set of four leather cuffs from the duffle and handed them to Ashleigh, her head bowed.

Jesse pushed through the crowd to the chain. Ashleigh fastened the cuffs around Rachel's wrists and ankles, then clipped them to the ends of four chains dangling from each arm of the cross. Stepping behind it, Ashleigh turned a crank that tightened the chains. Rachel stood with her ankles spread wide, her face where the upper arms of the cross met, and her arms stretched above her head.

Ashleigh reached into the bag and brought out two items he'd never seen before. Each had a braided leather handle and long, leather strands. At first, Ashleigh held one behind her back while she swirled the other one in a figure-eight pattern against Rachel's back. After a while, she twirled them together, gradually increasing her speed until the strands flew through the air, striking Rachel's back harder and harder.

Despite the force that Ashleigh used, Rachel didn't make a sound. Jesse could barely hear leather slapping flesh over the pulsing beat of The Pussycat Dolls' *Buttons*. He stared as Ashleigh stuffed the leather back in the bag and pulled out a long, narrow, wooden paddle. She stepped up to Rachel and ran her hand along the reddened skin of her back. She gripped Rachel's ass and put her mouth up to her ear. Ashleigh said something Jesse couldn't hear and Rachel nodded her head once.

Ashleigh stepped back, rubbed the paddle against Rachel's ass for a moment, then swung it. Jesse could tell she hit harder and harder with each stroke. She grabbed the paddle in both hands and landed a smack that Jesse heard over the music. Rachel flinched, but didn't cry out. Again and again, Ashleigh hit Rachel as hard as she could, a wicked grin on her face. She paused now between strokes. Rachel stood up on her toes, with clenched fists, after each blow. The moment she dropped her heels back to ground, Ashleigh swung again.

Jesse admired Rachel's stoicism, and wondered how much she could take. Her ass gleamed bright red in the dim light. When the song ended, Ashleigh stuck the paddle between her legs, reached around Rachel and grabbed her breasts. Jesse could see her talking into Rachel's ears, but he couldn't hear her words. When she released Rachel from the cross, Ashleigh sank down in front of it, holding Rachel in her arms. The two kissed, and Jesse felt himself swell despite having everything tucked between his legs in the gaff.

A big guy with tattoos all over his arms leaned over the chain and spoke to Ashleigh, but she shook her head. She pulled a thin blanket from the duffle, wrapped it around Rachel and helped her move to one side of the cross, kissing her forehead and propping her up against the wall. Then she looked up at Jesse and crooked a finger in his direction. Jesse stared at her wide eyed, unable to move. Ashleigh frowned and crooked her finger again. Despite his reluctance, he found himself stepping over the chain. Maybe she just needed him to get something for Rachel to drink.

Chapter Ten

When he walked up to Ashleigh, she unzipped his cincher. He gripped it against his waist and shook his head. Ashleigh held out her hand. Jesse relented and gave it to her. She added it to the pile of Rachel's clothing and held out her hand again. He knew what she wanted, but he couldn't imagine stripping in front of the nightclub crowd. Then he remembered the boy's head in the woman's lap, and how Ashleigh had held and kissed Rachel.

Jesse closed his eyes, crossed his arms, eased the dress up the length of his body, and pulled it over his head, handing it to Ashleigh. He could feel her moving around, but he couldn't open his eyes. He just knew people stared at him standing there, wearing just his gaff and his new boots. Jesse felt leather wrap around first one wrist and then the other. Ashleigh guided him with a gentle touch until he felt the cross against his chest. She lifted his arms, fastened the cuffs to the chains, and he heard the crank as his arms were pulled to the top of the cross.

Ashleigh pressed her breasts against his naked back, taking his breath away. "I need you to trust me, Jesse. I'm going to send you someplace you've never been, somewhere I think you'll enjoy. I'm going to start out slowly and build up until it hurts." She stepped back and drew the leather strands across his back. "This is a flogger. Some people compare getting flogged to a massage, but I can make it hurt, if I want." She reached around and pinched his nipple. Jesse wanted to crawl into a hole and die. Despite tape and confinement, the pain made him hard. "Tonight I'm going to hurt you, but you have the option of stopping me. If you yell out the word red, I'll stop immediately. That's your safeword. Do you understand?"

He nodded, even though he really didn't. What did she mean by a safeword? Why couldn't he just ask her to stop if he didn't like it?

She stood up on her tip toes and bit his earlobe. "But if you use the word red, I'll never play with you again." He could still feel her teeth in his ear, long after she released him. "You have to trust me Jesse. I know you need this, and I promise you'll thank me when I'm done."

He trembled. He'd seen what his best friend did to her lover, and the thought frightened him. Yet, something in her voice reached out to the hollow place inside him, the one that cried desperately to be filled. Sex hadn't done the trick. Maybe this would. He nodded, then leaned into the cross and waited.

Ashleigh stepped back and Jesse tensed. When he felt the flogger strands thud against his back, he relaxed just a little. It didn't really hurt. Ashleigh picked up the rhythm of the song flowing through the club's speakers, striking with the beat. Jesse took a deep breath. He let his sense of the room and whoever might be staring at him from the other side of the chain fade away. He became one with the Ashleigh's strikes against his back. If he looked down, he could see Rachel, still sitting cross-legged, leaning against the wall, wrapped in the blanket. When she looked up, her eyes didn't see him. She appeared totally stoned. Was that what Ashleigh meant by sending him someplace?

The flogger hit harder and harder, but it still didn't exactly hurt. Jesse rested his arms on the wood of the cross and concentrated on the feeling of the leather pummeling his back. He could smell it.

The strokes started to smart just a little. He thought about shouting red, but he found the pain tolerable. He also remembered Ashleigh's threat. He didn't know what she meant by playing with him, but Ashleigh and Rachel were his only friends. He needed them.

The pain became more intense. Again Jesse, thought about asking Ashleigh to stop, but he didn't want to disappoint her. She'd asked him to trust her. He clenched his jaw and his fists. He could feel tears forming behind his scrunched eyelids. The leather lashed him fast and furious now, with almost no time between when one stroke lifted from his back and the next one landed. Jesse let the pain wash over him. Even though the blows intensified, he found it interesting that the hurt really didn't. He dropped his head against his shoulder and hung from the cuffs around his wrist. Everything seemed fuzzy, as if he'd gotten drunk.

But, he couldn't remember anything like this, even when he and the girls polished off a bottle of peppermint schnapps on Rachel's birthday. Jesse wasn't sure when Ashleigh traded floggers for her paddle. He felt the blows. He thought they hurt, but he didn't care anymore. He just floated in euphoria.

When the paddle stopped and Ashleigh unfastened his wrists, he couldn't stand. She supported him, letting him slide to the ground next to Rachel. Emboldened by intoxication, he laid his head in Ashleigh's lap and much to his delight, she stroked his curls. An overpowering musk enveloped his nostrils, but he didn't pull away. He found it rather pleasant and snuggled closer, wrapping one arm around Ashleigh's waist. Someone pulled the cross away from them. A woman stood facing it with a man hitting her. Jesse thought about watching, but it didn't seem worth the effort of keeping his eyes open. He shivered and Ashleigh pulled a corner of Rachel's blanket over him. Rachel came with it and spooned him. He floated in bliss.

Chapter Eleven

Jesse woke on the plaid sofa in Ashleigh and Rachel's apartment, face down on the rough fabric. A black and red afghan covered him and it felt like their Siamese cat Pookie was curled up in the middle of his back. He couldn't remember leaving the club.

Bright sunlight poured in through the window above his head. He wore only the Spandex dress and his gaff. He needed to pee, and his crotch hurt from having everything tucked between his legs all night long. He tried to push himself up from the sofa, but Pookie howled. Afraid she'd wake Ashleigh and Rachel, Jesse dropped back down on his chest. He eased onto his side and Pookie eventually jumped down, flicking her tail at him in disgust.

He tiptoed to the bathroom, stripped off the gaffe and sat down, intending to pull off the tape. He almost jumped back up again, his ass hurt so much. When he finally got everything back out, he couldn't get a stream going, even though he felt as if he'd burst. He stood up, lifted the lid, and tried standing up to pee, something he usually only did when he wore jeans. He moaned softly in relief when things finally relaxed enough to work again.

After washing all the makeup off his face, Jesse went out to the living room and found his jeans and tee shirt. He hated wearing pants without underwear, but he didn't have tape with him and didn't want to try to get the gaff on without it. He'd deliberately purchased one too small, and it didn't fit well unless he tucked first. Retrieving his boots and cincher from on top of the leather duffle dropped by the front door, he returned them to the priority mail box and lay the dress on top of them. Jesse wondered if he should head home or wait for the girls to wake up. He looked at the clock on the pint-sized stove.

"Shit." He was gonna be late for class. His mother's histrionics when she learned he'd passed on U of O wouldn't compare to what she'd do if he got expelled from beauty college for missing class. She'd probably never forgive him. Maybe she'd never speak to him again. As tempting as that proposition seemed, Jesse didn't *want* to miss class. He ran down the stairs and sprinted for the bus stop.

He lowered himself into his seat one minute before the cutoff that would have gotten him marked late, earning a raised eyebrow from Ms. Johnston. Concentrating on class work proved more difficult than Jesse could have imagined. Although he'd regularly gotten drunk when he used to hang at Skinner Butte, he didn't remember ever being this hung over. The pain in his ass whenever he sat down didn't help. During his lunch break, Jesse walked down the block to Toshi's rather than follow his classmates across the street to McDonald's. He didn't think his stomach could manage a greasy burger and fries.

Normally, he brought his lunch, but this morning he hadn't had time to go home and fix something or even stop at a grocery store. At Toshi's, Jesse ordered a bowl of ramen noodles in miso, hoping it would stay down and not make him nauseous.

He felt a little better when he returned to school, although his head still ached and his stomach felt queasy. He wondered if someone had slipped him something.

While he tried to get his wig and rods ready for the class on perms, his schoolmate Lesley asked gave him a worried look. "You okay, Jesse?"

He tried to smile. "Guess I overindulged last night. Went out with some friends for a belated graduation celebration."

Lesley looked over her shoulder. "Have you tried drinking some Coke? That always helps me when I'm hung over."

He shook his head. She pulled a cup from the water cooler and filled it from the one-liter she always kept with her. Jesse was the only male in the class, and only Lesley and Cathie spoke to him more than absolutely necessary. Although he drank the Coke just to show appreciation for her kindness, he actually did feel better by the time the instructor started the class.

When they'd packed away their rods, chemicals, and supplies at the end of class, Jesse approached Lesley. "Hey, thanks for the Coke. It really helped."

She smiled. "So, where did you go to celebrate?"

"Devil's Den downtown."

Lesley had one arm in her linen jacket, and struggled to find the other sleeve. Jesse held it up by the collar to help her.

"Thanks." Barely five feet tall, she had blond hair that flowed down her back to her waist. She lifted it over her jacket collar. "Why Devil's Den? Didn't they have that icky fetish stuff last night?"

Jesse held the door leading outside for her. "That's where my friends took me. I enjoyed it."

Lesley raised one eyebrow. "They don't serve alcohol there, why exactly have you been fumbling around today?"

"Out too late. Sleep deprived, I guess." Jesse suspected lack of sleep only partially contributed to his hung-over feeling. But, if Lesley found the idea of fetish wear icky, he could just imagine what she'd think of him, bound naked, beaten with leather and wood by a lesbian. "But, hey, you only graduate from high school once, right?"

Lesley stared at him. "You just now getting around to celebrating? Wasn't graduation, like in June?

Jesse shrugged. "I graduated early, last month, actually."

She tilted her head and looked at him. "Do you mind if I ask how old you are?"

"Eighteen. Why?"

"Wow, I would have guessed more like sixteen. Had

no idea. Wondered how you got in to the school so young. Too bad you're gay. You're kinda cute."

"We could still go out for coffee sometime."

"Sure. McMenamins is less than four blocks from here. We can split a happy hour special. I don't know about you, but I'm starving."

Jesse mentally calculated how much money he had left after lunch. He could probably afford to share the price of an appetizer if he just ordered water to drink. "Sure, sounds like fun."

"Cathie," Lesley shouted at their classmate who stood leaning against the bus stop sign on the corner. "We're heading over to McMenamins. Wanna come?"

"Sure." Cathie, almost as tall as Jesse, towered over Lesley and weighed twice as much. Jesse had overheard other girls making fun of them, calling them Mutt and Jeff. He'd wondered if they were friendly to him because they were a couple. But that didn't make sense -- they were both femme. Even though Lesley usually wore jeans, she topped them with low-cut and frilly blouses and an embroidered jacket or pretty sweater. Today Cathie had on one of the shapeless dresses that seemed to make up her entire wardrobe. This one had big blue and green flowers against a dark background.

The three walked over to the burgundy and grey century-old house with covered front porch sheltered from the street by lattice panels.

Inside, Cathie slid into the only one of the high-backed wooden booths still empty. Lesley sat next to her and shrugged out of her jacket.

"Good timing." Cathie smiled and offered Jesse one of the paper menus strewn across the table. "Last booth."

He didn't take it. "Thanks, but I'm not really hungry. I can go in with you on something if you'd like."

"What can I get you folks?" A tall, bearded man wearing a green apron over a white shirt and blue jeans appeared at their table.

"Just water, please," Jesse said.

Cathie tossed the menu on the table."Terminator."

Lesley studied the menu for a moment. "Can I have a Hammerhead? And bring us all an order of black bean dip."

"May I see your ID, please." The man examined the proffered driver's licenses and then put three cork coasters on the table. "Coming right up."

A shout came from the long table in front of the fireplace and the waiter turned his back on them. Jesse wondered if he'd remember the order.

Cathie turned sideways, putting her back to the wall and one leg up on the bench seat. "So, what did you think of the perm class today?"

"Hate the smell." Lesley grimaced. "And, I don't understand why anyone would do that to their hair." She pulled a strand of her long, blond hair over her shoulder and twirled it.

"Not everyone has hair as nice as yours." Jesse wished his hair was that color. Instead, he had what most people described as dishwater blond -- not quite blond, not quite brown.

The server returned and put three large glasses on the table. The girls picked up theirs and held them out in Jesse's direction. He brought his water glass up to clink against their beers.

He took a sip. "You two are the only ones at school

who'll even speak to me. I wish I could afford to buy you both a beer."

Cathie turned so she faced Jesse and sat with her hands on either side of her beer glass. "I bet most of the other girls are hicks from Springfield, which explains why we're all outcasts. You're a nice kid, Jesse, but I think you'd do better in the business if you toned it down a little. Let's face it, you'll have a hard time getting a job if no one's sure whether you're male or female."

Jesse's lower lip trembled. "I'm male. I just prefer to wear feminine clothing."

"It's okay, really." Lesley patted his hand. "I mean, you probably wouldn't want to apply for a job in Springfield or Creswell, but this is Eugene." She elbowed Cathie. "Most people here are relatively tolerant."

Cathie smiled. "Hope so." She took a swig from her glass. "I mean, in a perfect world, no one'd give a shit. But we still live in the age of 'don't ask, don't tell'."

"Did you two vote against Measure 36?"

They both looked down, Cathie gripping her glass and Lesley turning a Celtic ring around and around on her middle finger. Cathie ran her fingers through her shoulder-length red hair. "Didn't vote."

Lesley shook her head. "Never got registered."

Jesse remembered what his mother said about young people not participating. He decided to get in touch with BRO again, to talk about campaigning for GLBT-friendly candidates running for the state legislature.

The server returned with a large bowl of bean dip on an oval plate with red, blue, and yellow tortilla chips. He set that in the middle of the table with a stack of napkins and three small plates next to it.

"Yum." Lesley spooned some dip onto a plate and dipped a chip in it. "Did you see the Ducks win the Civil War game last weekend?"

Cathie dipped a chip into the serving bowl. "Yeah, can't believe they won."

Jesse frowned. He knew the outcome. His dad, an OSU grad, always cheered his alma mater, despite living in Duck territory. But Jesse had no interest in discussing the finer points of the game, and he didn't like the way the girls had changed the subject.

Lesley crunched on a chip. "Yeah, Brooks and Crosswhite were in great form."

Jesse stared at her. The petite blonde didn't seem like the type who'd know the players' names and how well they'd scored. It seemed everyone in this town, with the exception of himself and his dad, worshiped the Ducks. Even Ashleigh and Rachel got excited about the games.

"Umm, could we not talk about basketball?" Jesse put a spoonful of the dip on a plate and scooped up some with one of the blue chips. "I'm the product of a mixed marriage, Duck Mom, Beaver Dad. Kind of a tense subject."

Cathie glowered at him. "And which are you?"

Jesse smiled. "Neither. Don't care much for any sports really. Except figure skating. I love watching the winter Olympics."

Cathie shook her head. "How can you live in Eugene and not care about the Ducks?"

Jesse shrugged. "One of the reasons I didn't think I'd fit in at U.O., even though I had a scholarship."

"Oh, like you fit in at the college." Lesley clapped her hand over her mouth.

"It's okay. I know what I'm up against. I've never really fit in anywhere." Not at Skinner Butte. Not in high school, despite serving as secretary of the Gay Straight Alliance and participating in the LGBT Youth Group. Besides his dad, Ashleigh and Rachel were the only two people in the world who accepted him exactly the way he was. And after last night, he even had to question his relationship with them. Still he liked where the pain sent him. He knew if Ashleigh asked him to strip down so she could beat him again, he wouldn't hesitate. What did that make him?

"I'm sure when you graduate, you'll do great." Cathie wiped her fingers on one of the napkins. "People'll put up with a lot of eccentricity if they like how a person does their hair." She pushed up her curls. "You gave me a great shampoo and set today."

Jesse smiled. They'd already started practicing on each other, and in a few weeks they'd get to spend their mornings working on the floor with actual customers. He'd signed up for the college at Ashleigh's urging, and because he saw no alternative. But, he found he really enjoyed hairstyling. "I hope you're right."

Lesley scraped the last of the dip from the bowl. "You just need to find the right shop. I bet Wild Roots would appreciate your talents."

Cathie nodded. "And, you don't have to worry about Christopher, he's totally out."

Jesse realized he really didn't know much about shops in Eugene. Probably should start researching sooner rather than later.

Chapter Twelve

The following Saturday, Ashleigh and Rachel took Jesse to a party with the weirdest mix of guests he'd ever seen. They ranged from his age to his grandparent's. Some of them wore fetish gear, although nothing as elaborate as he'd seen at Devil's Den. Others just had on plain jeans and shirts, and a few wandered around the house naked except for leather cuffs and collars.

Plates of finger food -- deviled eggs, sliced rollups, chicken wings, and cut up veggies -- covered the kitchen counter along with bowls of chips and plastic containers of dip. Rachel added the plate of cookies and sliced banana bread Ashleigh had instructed Jesse to make.

In the attached two-car garage, indoor/outdoor carpet covered the floor. An X-shaped cross stood against one wall, two folding massage tables were set up near the closed overhead door, and an odd shaped bench was positioned near the entrance to the house.

One wall was bare studs with dozens of protruding

eye hooks. He could also see hooks screwed into several of the ceiling beams. A naked man bound with leather cuffs had his back to the cross, and a shapely girl wearing only thigh-high stockings and stiletto heels was tied with rope to several of the eye bolts. Jesse remembered the agony and ecstasy of the weekend before, and was grateful this party was on Saturday rather than Sunday night. He'd have a day to recover before he returned to school on Monday.

Ashleigh sent Rachel to one of the massage tables, and turned to Jesse. "I'll come find you after my scene with Rachel. Go mix and mingle. Maybe you'll find a guy who strikes your fancy." Ashleigh winked.

Jesse smiled, but he'd have preferred to stay and watch whatever Ashleigh intended to do to Rachel. Still, the selection on the counter called to his empty stomach. He found a paper plate and loaded it with food. Someone had added a crockpot full of meatballs while he was in the garage. As he scooped some onto his plate, a raven-haired woman wearing black jeans and a black halter top held out her plate. He obliging added meatballs until she withdrew it.

She looked him over. "You're new here. Pretty, too. What's your name, boy?"

"Jesse." He felt he should add something to show his respect, but had no idea what.

She extended her left hand, palm down. "I'm Madame Sabrina. Does anyone own you, pretty boy?"

Jesse blushed. He'd worn the white dress with the polka dots and until she called him boy, he thought he passed pretty well.

"Oh, don't worry, my pretty." Madame Sabrina stood

up close and put her mouth next to his ear. She stood almost as tall as he, with a full figure he thought rather appealing. "I like cross dressers. But the Adam's apple always gives you away." She ran a finger along Jesse's throat and, much to his dismay, her touch excited him a little.

"Don't know that I'm really a cross dresser. I guess I think of myself more as a drag queen. I'm gay." That didn't fit either, but since she was apparently hitting on him, Jesse decided he'd better get his orientation out in the open. He added some potato chips to his plate and spooned some dip over them.

"Oh, sorry, my mistake." Madame Sabrina took her plate to the other side of the counter and struck up a conversation with an older woman who was trying to open a jar of gherkins.

Jesse wished he hadn't said anything. He wandered over toward the garage carrying his plate. Several people stood just inside the doorway watching a petite older woman hang small metal weights from the balls of the man cuffed to the cross. Nearby, another man flogged the girl tied to the wall. Jesse hoped that meant he could watch Ashleigh and Rachel without getting into trouble.

He sat down on the odd shaped bench near the entrance and ate one of the meatballs. It had a tangy sweet sauce, comfort food in the midst of all this exotic chaos. Naked, Rachel lay on her back on the massage table. Ashleigh attached clothespins, strung together on a black cord, to Rachel's breasts. Jesse wanted to get closer so he could see better, but he worried that Ashleigh would scold him. He stayed on the bench.

When Rachel's breasts bristled with clothespins,

Ashleigh ran one hand across the top of them. With her other hand, she used a thin, black, plastic rod to beat Rachel's shaved sex. Jesse stared, his plate forgotten in his hand. Rachel had one foot hanging off the table and he could see the folds between her legs opened wide. Moisture glistened on the red and swollen flesh. Ashleigh brought the rod up to Rachel's lips and made her lick it clean. Then she leaned over and kissed her.

"Are you going to use the spanking bench?" Madame Sabrina stepped in front of Jesse and blocked his view. A boy wearing a plaid school girl dress and a white blouse with long dreads tied in pigtails stood next to her, holding the handle of a rolling suitcase.

"I'm sorry, no, I was just sitting here." Jesse stood and moved along the wall, trying to get Rachel's crotch back into view.

"Dungeon furniture's for play, not seating," Madame Sabrina scolded.

"Yes, Ma'am. I'm sorry, Ma'am. I didn't know."

"That's better, boy." She pointed to the wall and the fellow in the skirt set the suitcase down and unzipped it. He knelt on the spanking bench, bending over, and flipping his skirt up over his waist. Madame Sabrina extracted a long, black wooden paddle from the suitcase and rubbed his ass with it. Then she drew back and swatted the boy with it.

"That's one, Ma'am. Thank you, Ma'am. May I have another?"

Madame Sabrina hit him again, and he repeated himself. Jesse turned back to the table in front of the garage door. Ashleigh had inserted a large purple dildo into Rachel. She pulled it out and pushed it in again.

Rachel moaned. Ashleigh pulled the dildo almost all the way out, took one end of the string attached to all the clothespins, and wrapped it around her hand. She yanked. Clothespins flew in every direction. Rachel screamed. Ashleigh jammed the dildo back inside of her at the same time and Rachel bucked her hips against Ashleigh's hand. Rachel cried out again, this time in a deep, guttural shout. She trembled all over and Ashleigh wrapped her in her arms.

The two women stayed that way. Jesse realized he'd cleared his plate, although he couldn't remember exactly when, so he returned to the kitchen looking for more food. Many of the containers were empty or nearly so. He found some cheese slices and took a couple of gherkins from the jar, then added more chips even though all the dip was gone. In the living room off the kitchen, folks sat on every available surface. A few even knelt on the carpeted floor or stood leaning against the wall. At one end of the room, an older woman with silver hair piled on top of her head held up with a pair of chopsticks sat in a leather armchair. She wore a flowing, tie dyed, kaftan-type dress. A bald, hairy fellow, naked except for rope wound around his chest in an intricate pattern, knelt in front of her and massaged her bare feet. Everyone in the living room seemed to know everyone else, except Jesse, and the conversation revolved around the Ducks' prospects in tomorrow's game and gossip about people he didn't know.

Jesse wandered back to the garage. Rachel now sat on the floor next to the table, wrapped in a blanket. Ashleigh held a container of cleaning wipes and was wiping off the table with one of them. The fellow on the cross probably had fifteen pounds hanging from his balls and the petite woman held some kind of electrical device near them. She ran the glass rod, glowing violet, over his pot belly and meaty thighs. It crackled with static electricity. He twitched and jerked.

The girl who'd been tied to the wall curled up on the floor in the arms of the man who'd flogged her. Madame Sabrina continued to paddle the cross dresser, even though his ass was bright red. "That's fifty-three, Ma'am. Thank you, Ma'am. May I have another."

Before he could make sense of any of it, Ashleigh caught Jesse's eye. She beckoned him over to the table and had him lie face down, flipping the skirt of his dress up over his back. With a half-inch thick, rattan pole about a yard long, she swatted his butt. At first her strokes just teased his flesh. But gradually, they got harder and harder. Eventually they bit into his ass and he expected he'd find welts when she finished.

As the pain became more intense, the floaty feeling he'd experienced the week before returned. He could feel every stroke of the rod on his rear, but the rest of the room -- the people in it, even the padded table under him -- disappeared from Jesse's consciousness. The pain from the repeated strokes on his flesh became his entire existence. Nothing else mattered, just the pain. The pain that seared his butt. The pain that sent him flying, but at the same time kept him grounded.

Jesse let go and fell into the pain. He let it carry him away to the euphoria he'd discovered only a week before. Already, he never wanted to live without it. Ashleigh placed a hand on his rear end and he lifted his pelvis into her caress. He dropped down again when, embarrassed, he realized he was hard as a rock. Laying face down on the table provided his only concealment. Fortunately, she didn't seem to notice. She just started her rhythmic beating on his ass again.

He wondered if he could rub against the table and get off. But Ashleigh would see the mess and he didn't want to embarrass her. Instead, he floated. He settled into the bliss and tried to ignore the pressure of laying on top of his erection and his almost overwhelming desire to stroke it.

When Ashleigh stopped and covered him with another blanket, Jesse hoped he could use it to hide how turned on he'd gotten. He wrapped the blanket around himself as he lifted up from the table and let Ashleigh guide him to the floor next to Rachel. Much to his surprise and delight, Rachel rested her head on his shoulder and let him wrap his arms around her. He floated in the euphoric aftermath of his beating, only vaguely aware of someone else screaming from the table until Ashleigh handed Rachel her clothes.

Jesse helped Rachel get dressed and the two followed Ashleigh out to the car, waiting as she said goodnight and hugged several folks on the way. She guided the car out into the empty residential street. "If I take you home, will you be okay or do you need to sleep on our sofa again?"

Jesse didn't want to go home to his parents' house, but left alone he could masturbate and relieve the need that sitting on his sore ass reignited. "I think I can manage on my own."

As soon as Ashleigh drove away from his parents' house, he regretted his decision. Rummaging through his purse, he couldn't find his house key. When he finally dug it out, he had trouble inserting it into the lock. For some reason, the door handle wouldn't stay still and he couldn't think of anything to do about it. Once inside, Jesse's only concern was not waking his parents. He crept through the living room and up the stairs toward the bedrooms.

When he managed to close the door to his room, he leaned against it and slid to the floor. He reached under his skirt and pulled his gaffe out far enough so he could get his hand between his legs to remove the tape. Although pulling it off hurt, when he finally got his cock free of its bindings, he only wanted to stroke it.

He ran his hand up and down his cock, pulling the skin back and forth. He propped his knees up and reached with one hand to drag his fingernails across his butt to reawaken the agony from Ashleigh's welts. With the help of the pain and the memory of Rachel's moist, quivering flesh in his mind, he got off almost immediately. Unable to even conceive of a way of getting up from the floor, Jesse fell over on to his side, pulled his knees up to his chest, and went to sleep with his back against the door.

Chapter Thirteen

Only his dad attended his graduation from beauty school. Ashleigh had to work and Rachel had gone up to Seattle for a week. Neither told him why, and he worried that the two of them might break up. His mother claimed to have a headache, and sent his dad in to his room to break the news. Jesse knew she just couldn't bear to see her gay son receive his certification as a hair designer.

Jesse had found a stunning blue and black sequined sheath at the thrift store for only fifteen dollars and matched it with a lovely pair of black patent leather pumps. He knew he was overdressed, even for an evening ceremony, but he'd worked hard to earn the piece of paper the head of the school would hand him. He hadn't told his dad he was graduating first in his class. He wanted to surprise him.

"You ready, son?" His dad stood in the doorway of his bedroom. "My, don't you look just sensational."

Jesse smiled and twirled around, showing off the slit

on the side that ran from his knee halfway up his thigh. "Isn't it just the most lovely dress?"

"Well, you do it justice, son. You know we're both very proud of you."

Jesse accepted his dad's use of the plural pronoun, even though he understood that he really only shared his own feelings. "Thanks, Dad." His mother would never be proud of him, would never accept him. Jesse put the strap of the small black satin purse over his shoulder and followed his dad out of the house.

At the school, most of the students avoided him, as usual. Neither Lesley or Cathie had completed their requirements yet, so they had no reason to attend.

"Goodness! You look absolutely lovely, Jesse." Ms. Johnston, his favorite teacher offered her hand to his dad. "Is this your sweetheart?"

His dad cleared his throat and Jesse blushed. "Ma'am, this is my dad, Bob. Dad, this is Ms. Johnston, the greatest teacher in the entire school."

Ms. Johnston actually blushed. "You sweetie! You are my very best student, and I know you'll do quite well. Have you found a job yet?"

"Yes, at Shear Perfection over on Eleventh." After getting turned down at half a dozen studios, Jesse had changed his resume, removing all references to his participation in LGBT activities, despite teacher assurances that extra curricular activities would help students get jobs. He'd also left gender blank on the application and said nothing when the owner marked it female during the interview.

"Oh, you'll love working with Betsy. She graduated from here longer ago than I'll bet she's willing to admit."

One of the other students tapped Ms. Johnston on the shoulder. "You'd best go take your seat, Jesse. We start soon."

Jesse tried to enter one of the two rows of folding chairs reserved for the fifteen graduates to make his way to the empty seats in the middle. The girls all moved down so two empty chairs now remained on the aisle. With a sigh, Jesse sat in the first one, leaving an empty chair between him and the rest of his class.

He found his mind wandering while Ms. Lawrence, the school director rambled on about responsibilities and career opportunities. He started paying attention when Ms. Johnston brought the stack of certificates up to the podium and handed one to Ms. Lawrence. "It's with great pride that I award the first certificate this evening to the top student in his class, Richard Jesse Andrews. This young man had perfect grades in all but one of his classes, and had the highest scores on his state examination ever achieved by a student from this college."

Jesse walked up to the podium to polite applause from the teachers and parents. His fellow students sat with their hands in their laps.

Ms. Lawrence handed him his diploma and his state certificate both of which had only his middle name as he'd requested. "Congratulations Jesse. You worked very hard, and I'm sure you'll be quite successful."

Jesse shook Ms. Lawrence's hand and returned to his seat. On his way back, his dad caught his eye and mouthed *I'm so proud*. Jesse smiled. At least one person in the room cared about his achievements.

Chapter Fourteen

When Rachel returned from Seattle, the girls threw him a graduation party. Jesse recognized many of those attending from various fetish events. Plates of cookies, chips and dip, cold cuts, cocktail franks in tomato sauce, and carrot sticks filled the kitchen counter and the small metal table. Each time a new guest arrived, someone scrambled to make room for whatever they brought.

Many of the women asked for his card. Jesse hadn't thought to have any made, so he collected e-mail addresses and promised to send everyone information about where he was working.

When there didn't seem room enough for another person in the small apartment, Ashleigh brought out a sheet cake decorated with a blue scissors and "Congratulations Jesse!" She set the cake on a chair and Rachel handed Jesse a box.

"We decided to take up a collection rather than have

you get a lot of little gifts you don't need. This is from everyone here."

Jesse's hands trembled as he took the slender package. Inside the silver paper, he found a leather case that unzipped to reveal a pair of sky blue Katana shears, a styling razor and comb. He'd saved every penny he had, trying to put together enough to buy an inexpensive set, figuring he could buy quality once he got established. He knew the tools he held in his hand cost at least three hundred dollars online. A tear rolled down his cheek.

"Thank you all so much. These are just beautiful. I'm ..." Jesse gave up trying to speak and just let the tears flow. Ashleigh and Rachel embraced him in a group hug, each planting a kiss on his cheek. When they released him, everyone else in the room converged and he got hugs and kisses from people he barely knew. He had to remind himself that these people accepted him for who he was and cared enough about him to chip in on his amazing present. He suspected Ashleigh and Rachel provided the bulk of the cost and he promised himself they would never pay for haircuts again.

Once the excitement subsided, Rachel handed him a knife. Jesse cut pieces of the cake and handed them around.

Ashleigh pointed to a muscular man in his late twenties wearing a leather vest and leather chaps over black jeans. "And this is Tony." He had a horseshoe through his septum, zero gauge talons in both ears, two lippy loops through his bottom lip, an eyebrow ring over his left eye, and a tribal tattooed on his left bicep. Black and light blue bandanas hung out of his back left pocket and he wore his black hair in a buzz cut.

Tony slipped his fingers into Jesse's hair and tugged his neck backward until he dropped to his knees. Tony stepped close and leaned down to Jesse's ear. "I understand you like to fly," he whispered. Time you stop playing with girls, pretty boy, and learn where a man can send you."

Jesse winced but said,"Yes, Sir." The smell of leather filled his nostrils.

"I'm going to find out what you're made of, pretty boy. I'll take you places these girls don't even know about."

Jesse just wanted Tony to release his hair before he got a crick in his neck. Someone from across the room called Tony's name. Jesse got his wish and scrambled to his feet. He spent the rest of the party staying as far away from Tony as he could. Everyone else seemed to gravitate toward the man. Men and women crowded close to him, vying for his attention, touching his arm.

⌣J

When all the guests finally left, Jesse pulled out a large green trash bag and gathered up paper plates and cups left on top of bookcases, the coffee table, and on the floor behind the couch. He covered all the leftover food in cling wrap and put it away before he wiped the counter and table with a damp rag. When he was done, he turned around to find Ashleigh and Rachel sitting next to each other on the sofa, staring at him.

"We have something we need to tell you, Jesse." Ashleigh had one arm draped over Rachel's shoulder.

Jesse felt the hairs on the back of his neck stand on

end. He knew he didn't want to hear what they had to say. "Kind of late. Can this wait 'til tomorrow?"

"No." Ashleigh pointed to one of the kitchen chairs. "Take a seat."

Jesse swallowed, pulled the chair across from the couch and turned it to face them.

"First, you need to expand your S&M experiences." Ashleigh pulled Rachel tighter under her arm. "There're some things I just won't do with a guy. I've asked Tony to take your education to the next level."

Jesse closed his eyes and shook his head.

"Second," Ashleigh continued without acknowledging his protest. "Rachel and I are moving to Seattle. I got the store manager's position in Auburn and Rachel went up last week to find a job. I start a week from Tuesday and she's already given her two weeks' notice here."

Jesse couldn't breathe. He felt tears streaming down his face for the second time that evening, but these made his chest ache and his head hurt. "You guys can't leave me."

Ashleigh patted Jesse's knee. "I've asked Tony to watch over you. It makes more sense for you to be with him anyway."

Jesse shook his head.

"Good grief, boy." Rachel scowled. "How long since you've had sex anyway? At least this way, you can get beat and laid, both."

Jesse wanted to say no. He was perfectly happy without sex. But he couldn't get any words out. He dropped to his knees in front of Ashleigh and put his head in her lap.

Ashleigh stroked his hair. "You'll like Tony once you

get to know him. Everybody does. And, he'll introduce you to CBT. I suspect you'll enjoy that a lot."

Wrapping his arms around Ashleigh's waist, Jesse just sobbed. He'd struggled in school, trying to find a friend. Finally he'd given up and concentrated on his studies instead. On Tuesday, he started working where he had to pretend to be female. He knew better than to try to get close to anyone at the beauty shop. How would he survive without the only real friends he'd ever had?

Ashleigh pulled his head up by his hair. "You'll be okay, Jesse. Really. You'll have Tony and his boys to hang out and go to parties with. You shouldn't spend all your time with a couple of dykes anyway. Just doesn't make sense. Don't you get horny?"

Not horny enough to want to get fucked by someone who could set off the airport metal detector naked. Jesse shook his head, his movement limited by Ashleigh's grip on his hair.

She laughed. "Oh, good grief, of course you do." Ashleigh released Jesse's hair and stood up. "You'd better head home. We start packing first thing in the morning". She walked over to the table and picked up the leather case. "Hope you enjoyed your party."

Jesse accepted the case, but he still couldn't speak without bursting into tears again. He clutched it to his chest. He'd always treasure their gift, but it also would always remind him that they'd abandoned him.

"Here, why don't you take the rest of the cake? We sure don't need it." Rachel retrieved the cake box from under the table, settled the cardboard platter that still held a third of the sheet cake into the box, and handed it to Jesse.

"I gave Tony your phone number and e-mail." Ashleigh held open the door to the apartment. "He'll get in touch. You take care, boy." She touched her palm to his cheek.

Jesse handed the cake box to Rachel and hugged Ashleigh. She pushed him away after only a few seconds. With the leather case balanced on top of the cake box, Jesse fumbled his way down the stairs.

Chapter Fifteen

The first time Tony called, Jesse answered his phone thinking someone from the beauty shop needed to get hold of him. He begged off the invitation to come over to Tony's house with the excuse that he'd already made plans. Jesse checked out Tony's MySpace profile, and discovered he had five hundred and eighty-five friends. Scanning the comments on his wall and his blogs, Jesse couldn't understand the appeal. The man couldn't spell and his acquaintance with the English language seemed distant at best. His posts ridiculed folks involved in politics, sports, and entertainment.

Jesse programmed Tony's number into his phone and selected the silent option so his calls wouldn't ring. That pretty much meant Jesse's phone stayed quiet. Neither Ashleigh or Rachel returned his calls, although they did respond to his messages on MySpace. Besides them and Tony, only his parents and Betsy had the number.

Jesse showed up at work every day precisely on time,

so Betsy never had any reason to call him. She gave his customers, with their brightly colored hair and body modifications, disdainful looks. None of them came back after one visit and Betsy chastised him for not bringing in enough business.

Nicole, who worked in the mayor's office and refrained from piercing or tattooing anything she couldn't cover with clothing, came in a second time. "This place is so depressing," she complained while Jesse snipped away.

He cringed. Her voice carried to the front of the shop where Betsy sat behind the cash register.

"Why don't you go work someplace fun?" She winked at Jesse in the mirror and he wondered what she had up her sleeve. "Most of the girls would come back to you if you weren't in this abysmal place. They loved how you cut and colored their hair. They just can't abide this dump." Nicole stuck one hand out from under the plastic cape and waved it dramatically.

Jesse leaned down and whispered in her ear. "Please, Nicole. You'll get me fired."

She looked up at him. "That would be a good thing." Fortunately, she kept her voice low. "Wild Roots is hiring and we already talked to Christopher about you. We told him you come with at least a dozen loyal customers. He'd be delighted to have you and you wouldn't have to pretend there, either."

"But, you're the only customer who's asked for me in two weeks." Jesse's only ladies were walk ins and people who called from the phone book. He barely made his second month's apartment rent.

"Sweetie." Nicole raised her voice again. "All the girls would just flock back to you if you worked someplace that wasn't so icky. They didn't stop coming to you. They stopped coming to this crummy place."

Jesse finished trimming Nicole's hair and brushed away bits of hair from her shoulders. He pulled out a pair of gloves, but she stopped him from putting them on. "Don't bother with the highlights. I can't stand this place that long, either."

He swallowed, but removed the brown plastic cape. Nicole handed him folded up fives, covering the cost of her haircut. In the middle he found a card for the Wild Roots Salon. "You're better than this place, Mister Andrews."

Jesse wanted to sink through the floor into oblivion. He could feel all color draining from his cheeks. "Why?" He'd made sure all the friends who came to the shop knew that Betsy thought he was female.

Nicole stood up on her tiptoes and planted a kiss on Jesse's cheek. "Because we've conspired against you. I've been appointed to get you out of this place so you can take care of our hair." She turned and headed for the door, stopping to lean on the counter in front of Betsy. "This place is disgusting. I won't be back."

Sweeping up the blond hair clippings, Jesse tried to keep from bursting into tears. He appreciated Nicole's and the others' concern. He hated coming to this shop every morning, worrying that one of his co-workers would discover his secret, washing the hair of little old ladies who came in once a week and never shampooed at home. But he'd applied at Wild Roots before he graduated and was told they only hired people with experience. He doubted six weeks would make a big difference there.

After he emptied the hair into the waste basket, he

looked up to see Betsy glowering at him from the front counter. "I'll take that money, and then you can pack up your things. I don't need the kind of riff raff you attract in my shop."

Jesse extracted the business card and handed over the bills to Betsy. He sanitized his sheers and comb, dried them off with paper towels, and stuck them back in the leather case. Removing his framed certificates from the wall above his station, he collected his purse, and slunk out of the shop. He walked to the bus stop, but he'd just missed the four ten. Jesse extracted his cell phone from his purse and looked at the card Nicole had given him.

Sitting down on the bench, he set his certificates next to him and dialed the salon number. "May I speak to Christopher, please?" he asked the woman who answered the phone.

"I'm sorry, he's doing a perm. If I can take your number, he'll call you back."

Yeah, right. Jesse thought to himself. But he gave her his name and number and waited for the bus.

When he got home to his one-room apartment, Jesse took stock of his situation. He had three weeks before he had to pay rent again. He probably had enough food to last a week. His cell phone bill didn't come due until the end of the month. "You could just turn that off. It's not like anyone calls you," he said aloud. Jesse buried his face in his arms and waited for the tears, but he couldn't mourn the loss of a job he hated. Tomorrow he'd head over to Valley River Center and see if he couldn't get something in one of the stores there. Maybe one of the managers at Hot Topics would remember him as a friend of Ashleigh's and hire him.

Chapter Sixteen

ickelback's "Rockstar" startled Jesse to his feet. His phone. He grabbed his purse and dumped it out onto the table. He opened the phone without taking time to look at the number. "Hello?"

"This Jesse?"

"Yes."

"Christopher, from Wild Roots. You called?"

Jesse took a deep breath. "Nicole mentioned that you might have an opening?"

"Nicole?"

Jesse's hopes fell.

"Wait, are you the stylist Tony's been trying to get me to hire? 'Bout time you called. When can you start?"

Jesse's eyes widened. He hated the idea of being in the man's debt, but he needed a job and he doubted anyone at the mall would hire him, anyway. "Tomorrow?"

"Great. Tony said you'd bring your own following, so if you can get here first thing in the morning, I'll let you use the computer to broadcast to your e-mail list. Then we can update the website."

Shear Perfection didn't even have an e-mail address, never mind a website. "Yes, Sir, what time would you like me to get there?"

"We open at ten, so why don't you show up around nine-thirty and I can get you set up with a logon. Make sure you bring your list on flash."

"Yes, Sir. Thank you, Sir."

"Just call me Christopher, okay? See you tomorrow."

"Sir, Christopher, could I ask you one question?" Jesse waited for a response, but Christopher had ended the call. Jesse had no idea what to wear to work in the morning.

He booted his computer and searched for the Wild Root's website. The photographs reminded him that the salon had brightly painted walls, modern chairs, and new fixtures. Christopher's picture showed an androgynous forty-something with shaggy, razor cut black hair and long bangs. The only other male pictured on the site had long straight blond hair tied back in a ponytail. The photos only showed faces, no clothing.

Searching the Internet, Jesse found a couple of articles about the shop's opening eight years ago, listings for it on the sponsor page of the Eugene Springfield Pride Festival, and Christopher's name listed on the board of directors of the Q Center. Neither Christopher or Wild Roots had a MySpace page, but Christopher was on Friendster.

None of the information helped Jesse figure out what to wear in the morning. He poked through his closet, pulling out and rejecting everything he owned. Finally, he decided on a silky pink blouse and a pair of white, linen slacks. *Not too femme, not too butch.* Smiling, he ironed a couple of wrinkles out of the blouse and hung both up on the hook screwed to the bathroom door. He rummaged through his shoes and found a pair of white, Doc Marten ankle-high boots he thought would work.

While heating a frozen pot pie in the oven, Jesse sat at the table and stared at his phone. He needed to call Tony and thank him. He paged through the missed calls and counted sixteen. He sighed and pushed send. Jesse let out his breath in relief when he reached Tony's voicemail.

"Hey, Tony, I just talked to Christopher over at Wild Roots. I wanted to thank you *so* much for putting in a good word for me. I really appreciate it. See you around." Jesse pressed the pound sign and waited for the menu option that would let him listen to his message. He played it twice before he decided he could live with it and chose the normal delivery option.

He checked the timer. Twenty more minutes. He went to find his flash drive so he could download the e-mail addresses he'd collected at his graduation party.

Chapter Seventeen

Christopher fit every stereotype of the gay hairdresser. He waved his hands around as if they were attached by straps. He called all the customers "darling," and his shirt made Jesse's look positively butch. However, Wild Roots pulsed with music from NRQ, Jesse recognized the celebrities in the glamour pictures on the walls, and the customers, as well as the staff, had piercings and tattoos.

Jesse had no difficulty writing the e-mail he sent to everyone he knew, and Christopher praised his enthusiasm.

"My dear friends." Jesse realized most of the people on his list wouldn't consider him a friend. But he so appreciated this opportunity, he was ready to embrace them all. "I'm very excited to let you know I've joined the amazing team of stylists and technicians at Wild Roots downtown. I know many of you didn't appreciate the atmosphere at my last location or the discretion required when visiting there. I hope you'll all come see me at Wild Roots and discover just how much fun you can have while getting your hair and nails done. Anyone who mentions this e-mail (until the fifteenth of next month) will receive a ten percent discount off any services they purchase from me."

When Christopher suggested the discount, Jesse worried how much that would cut into his income. Betsy only paid him half of what he brought in. Subtract another ten percent, and he'd still have a hard time making his rent, even if all the customers who couldn't abide Shear Perfection patronized him at Wild Roots.

"May I ask what percentage you normally pay your stylists and how much you charge for a basic cut?"

Christopher laughed. "I pay my stylists by the hour, dear boy. If you don't have anyone in the shop, I don't permit you to sit around on your pretty little ass and file your nails. There's always work that needs doing, especially marketing. I want you to double the size of your mailing list in the next ninety days, and I expect you to send out some kind of announcement to it at least once a month."

He handed Jesse a filled, purple, three-ring binder. "This is the employee manual. I expect you to read it all. The price lists are in there, as well as sample e-mail letters and some examples of promotions I've offered in the past. Coupons and discounts are a cost of doing business, not something to take out of the stylist's pocket. You start at fifteen an hour, but you can earn bonuses by increasing your product sales and raises by expanding your customer base."

Jesse sat stunned for a moment. Then he added another line to the e-mail before sending it. "Please share this e-mail with anyone you know who might be interested in having me cut, color, or perm their hair. Referrals are always greatly appreciated." He needed to devise a way for the girls who liked how he did their hair to get rewarded for referring new clients.

⌒J

Nicole came in that afternoon to get her highlights. "Isn't this place so much better?"

Jesse wrapped her in a bright purple micro fiber cape and pulled on a pair of gloves. "I'm so incredibly grateful. I'm really excited about working here. Christopher seems like a great boss." Unlike his previous employer, who'd deducted every cost related to his station from his paycheck.

"Well, you really need to thank Tony. Christopher doesn't usually hire anyone with less than a year's experience. He prefers more. But Tony got everyone to promise we'd bring you our business and convinced Christopher to make an exception."

Jesse busied himself mixing the tint and blinked his eyes to keep the fumes from burning them. He knew the tears he fought were as much in response to the thought of what Tony might expect in return as from the chemicals. He pulled strands of Nicole's hair on top of a sheet of foil and brushed on the tint. "That certainly was kind; I barely know him."

Nicole laughed. "You know Ashleigh and Rachel expect him to watch out for you. He's always asking about you."

Jesse managed to smile, but Nicole's revelation made him wonder just how much this new job was worth. He folded up the foil and reached for another piece. Perfect working conditions. Divine boss. Good pay. A chance to build up a real clientele in exchange for dating a good-looking leatherman who claimed he could send Jesse flying. He tried to convince himself that there was no downside. He knew what Ashleigh would tell him, but Jesse wondered if he would ever find any man attractive enough to enjoy sex with him.

Once he had all of Nicole's foils in, he led her over to the cushy dryer chairs, unlike the cheesy rollabout dryers at Shear Perfection. As instructed in the employee manual, Jesse offered to get Nicole a beverage and found the one she requested in the fridge. While her color processed, he cleaned up his station and tried to figure out what he wanted in a man. He thought of all the guys he'd dated. Maybe if he took Marc's looks combined with David's kindness, and added Tony's willingness to beat him ...

Jesse turned off Nicole's dryer and led her over to one of the shampoo stations. "I thought Tony had someone." He tried to keep his voice casual, gingerly removing the hot aluminum foil and dropping it in the bin.

Nicole tilted her head. "He's poly. Haven't you dated him at all?"

"I just met him that one time at the party." He guided her head back so her neck rested against the sink.

Nicole didn't try to continue the conversation over the running water, and Jesse avoided looking at her face while he shampooed, rinsed, and conditioned her hair. But as soon as he turned off the water, she spoke.

"I think you need to have a conversation with Tony. He seems to think that Ashleigh and Rachel gave you to him and that he owns you now. He certainly speaks of you as if you were one of his boys."

Back at his station, Jesse concentrated on combing tangles out of her hair, then reached for the blow dryer to stop the conversation. While he styled Nicole's hair, Jesse glanced around at the lovely salon -- the latest equipment and furniture, stylish, not worn out stuff from the eighties. No one expected him to pretend he was female here. On the other hand, he expected no one would give him grief about wearing girls' clothing, either. According to Nicole, he could expect to stay quite busy. Nothing could be more perfect, so if he had to serve as Tony's sex slave in return ... what was so awful about that? Especially if Tony made him fly. He hadn't experienced subspace since Ashleigh left. He missed the euphoria.

Turning off the blow dryer, Jesse stuck it in the holder on the side of his station, then turned the chair around so Nicole faced the mirror.

She smiled when she saw her reflection. "Lovely as always, sweetie."

"Only because I have such beautiful hair to work with and it just pales in comparison to the gorgeous woman it belongs to." Jesse pulled a stray hair back into position. The stylists at Shear Perfection would gush all kinds of platitudes to even the ugly old ladies who came in every week for a shampoo and set. Jesse only gave genuine compliments. Fortunately, that wouldn't prove difficult for the women he hoped would follow him to Wild Roots.

"You are such a doll." Nicole reached for her purse and extracted a Visa card. "I love having you do my hair, and I'm so very glad I don't ever have to go back to Shear Torture."

Jesse snickered. He took the plastic, apparently another advantage of working at Wild Roots -- Betsy only accepted cash and checks. At the front desk, Christopher appeared from nowhere. "Let me show you how we do that here."

When he returned to hand Nicole her card, the charge slip, and a pen, Jesse watched in astonishment as she added a twenty percent tip. When he saw the price list, he'd worried that some of his friends might not be able to pay Wild Root's much higher rates or that they might compensate by cutting back on his tips. He wouldn't have blamed them.

Nicole handed him the slip and the pen. "This place puts me in a much better mood. And, you're worth it." She smiled.

Overwhelmed, Jesse took her hand and touched his lips to her fingers.

"Ooo, that's just perfect for here." Nicole kissed his cheek and headed out of the salon, waving to Christopher as she left.

Chapter Eighteen

Jesse unpacked the groceries he'd picked up on his way home. With a promise of a full paycheck in two weeks, he'd splurged on fresh produce and meat. On his second trip to the fridge, he saw his phone flashing on the counter. It reminded him that he needed to change Tony's setting back to a ring. This time, he answered it.

"So, how'd the first day go, boy?"

"Great, Tony. I can't begin to thank you enough for helping me get this job. I just love Wild Roots. It's a fabulous place to work. Christopher's an amazing boss. He uses better quality products, has newer equipment, and treats his employees so much nicer than Betsy ever did. I'm very, very grateful."

"Oh, I'm sure you can figure out a way to show me just how grateful you are."

Jesse's entire face scrunched up in a grimace.

"Whatcha doing right now?"

"Fixing dinner."

"Well, make enough for two. I'll be there in forty-five minutes."

"Yes, Sir."

Jesse stared at the phone in his hand. After a deep sigh, he changed the ringtone for Tony's entry in his contacts and set the phone back on the counter. Wiping the back of his hand under his eyes to push back the tears that threatened to spill out, he wrapped the chicken and ground beef he'd just purchased in the plastic bag and tucked it in the very back of the fridge. He washed the fruit and stuck it in a bowl, that he put on top of the fridge, not inviting, but not inaccessible. Then he dug out a pot and filled it with water.

By the time Tony arrived, Jesse had boiled spaghetti and heated bottled sauce. In his only concession to having a guest in the house, he tossed a green salad with balsamic vinaigrette.

When Jesse opened the door, Tony said "Smells good." He wore a black tee shirt and a black denim Utilikilt. He dropped his knapsack on the floor, grabbed Jesse by the hair, and pulled him to his knees. "Learn how to greet me properly, boy." Tony leaned down and planted a kiss on Jesse's forehead.

"Yes, Sir." Jesse pointed to the small round table and mismatched chairs that he'd scored from Eugene Free Recycle. "Dinner's ready."

Tony left him kneeling by the door, swung a leg over one of the chairs and plopped down. Jesse stumbled to the stove, heaped a plate with spaghetti, and poured sauce on it. When he set it in front of his guest, Tony had already taken most of the salad from the bowl on the table and piled it on the smaller plate Jesse had put out.

"Would you like something to drink. I'm afraid I only have Mountain Dew and water."

Tony swallowed a mouthful of greens. "Mountain Dew's fine." He spun his fork in the spaghetti, twirling the strands into a ball, and stuffing it in his mouth. "Not bad, could use some meat, though."

Jesse busied himself finding a glass and pouring Mountain Dew from the two-liter in the fridge. He fixed himself a small portion of spaghetti, sat down across from Tony, and picked at his food.

"Need to eat more than that, boy. Put some meat on those bones." Tony scraped the remaining sauce from his plate then stared at Jesse while he picked at his food.

When he could no longer stand the scrutiny, Jesse picked up both plates and took them to the sink. "Bit stressed lately, although I expect things'll get much better now that I'm at Wild Roots."

"Mmmph. I think I know why you're stressed, boy. When's the last time anyone gave you a proper beating?"

Jesse wondered if he could even hope that was all Tony would offer. "Not since Ashleigh and Rachel left."

"That's what I thought. How come you never got back to me, boy? I left you at least half a dozen messages."

Jesse shrugged and rinsed off the plates. "Kind of busy." He could feel Tony's eyes on his back. He tried to think of a way to extract himself from his dilemma and then questioned why he wanted to.

"Well, I'm here now. You can do the dishes later. Bring me my pack."

Jesse rinsed off his hands and wiped them slowly on a dish towel. The distance from door to sink had somehow tripled and the weight of the pack seemed unbearable.

When Jesse set the pack in front of him, Tony unzipped the large front pocket and withdrew a long, buffalo-hide flogger, a four-foot signal whip, a set of leather wrist cuffs, and a metal piece Jesse didn't recognize.

"You clean boy?" Tony tilted his head.

"I took a shower this morning."

Tony laughed. "That's not what I meant, fool. Been tested for HIV?"

Jesse swallowed. So much for hope. He wanted to lie, but he feared the consequences. "Not for a six months or so, Sir, but I haven't had sex since then."

Tony attached the metal piece to the top of the bathroom door and closed it. "Six months? Beating's not the only thing you're overdue for." He fingered the six-inch sheathed knife on his belt. "You still have clothes on boy, you want me to cut that pretty shirt off you?"

"No, Sir. I'll be right back."

Jesse turned for the bathroom door, but Tony grabbed his hair. "You can take your clothes off right here, boy. Make it good for me."

Tony threw one leg over the chair again, but this time he faced its back. He rested his chin on the vinyl padding, watching Jesse slowly unbutton his blouse. He wasn't trying to tease. He just couldn't get his trembling fingers to work any faster. He closed his eyes as the blouse slipped off his shoulders and tossed it in the direction of the futon sofa that doubled as his bed. Jesse tried to reassure himself that Ashleigh wouldn't have picked Tony to watch over him if she didn't trust the man. But, Tony had never asked if he wanted sex or a flogging or any kind of relationship. Still, Tony *had* gotten him an amazingly perfect job.

Jesse unbuttoned and unzipped his slacks, lowering them to his ankles with his pink satin panties. He stepped out of them and dropped them on top of his blouse.

Tony held out a cuff. Not knowing how to resist without upsetting Tony, Jesse trudged over to him and set his wrist on the padded leather.

Once he'd buckled the cuffs around Jesse's wrists, Tony brought them up over his head and clipped them to the hook he'd attached to the bathroom door. Tony ran his hands all over Jesse's ass, up his sides, and down his chest. He teased Jesse's cock and much to his surprise he actually rose to the occasion. Maybe Tony was the one. He tried to relax.

Tony warmed him up with the flogger. Jesse let go and enjoyed the slap of the leather on his back. The first kiss of the single tail set him free and each subsequent sting stripped away more of his resentment. He lost track of time and how often leather struck flesh. By the time the whip started to build welts, Jesse flew and wondered how he'd lived without this the last few weeks. Through the euphoria, he realized Tony had stopped throwing the whip. He felt the heat of the man's body pressed up against his own.

"Your back can't take much more, boy, and I don't have time to do a proper CBT scene tonight." Tony's hands roamed everywhere on Jesse's body, taking possession of his property. "But, you look like you'll do fine with what I've given you. Right, boy?"

"Yes, Sir." His legs too weak to support him any longer, his wrists tired from the pull of the cuffs, he leaned back into Tony's embrace.

Tony kissed his neck and bit his ear. Jesse moaned. Tony pushed him into the door. He could feel a hard cock pressed against his welted ash cheeks. He couldn't remember Tony removing his own clothing, but he could feel the other man's skin along his entire length. Tony reached up and unclippped the cuffs from the hook. Jesse let Tony take his weight and drag him to the futon sofa. Tony kissed him, hard. He opened his lips and let Tony invade his mouth, a hint of garlic mingling with the sweet tang of Mountain Dew. Tony could have whatever he wanted. Jesse didn't care about anything except floating in the exquisite elation of subspace.

Tony stuck his cock in Jesse's mouth, and he sucked on it without protest. Willing to do almost anything to continue his flight, Jesse let Tony face fuck him and spurt all over his chest. When Tony held come-covered fingers up to Jesse's mouth, he obediently licked them clean. He had to admit Tony's come tasted better than any other man's, although he still didn't like it.

"Good boy." Tony pulled the blanket from the corner of the sofa and covered Jesse with it. "Gotta go. I'll see you tomorrow."

Jesse's head lolled to one side. "Fly high, pretty boy." Tony kissed him again and somewhere from the fog surrounding his brain, Jesse heard the click of the apartment door close.

Chapter Nineteen

Jesse never converted the sofa, nor did he have presence of mind to set an alarm. He woke to discover he had less than forty-five minutes to get to work. Scrambling to get dressed, he threw on the first things his fingers found in his closet: a black pleated skirt and white blouse. He couldn't even spare a moment to put on any makeup, barely having time to wash his face and scrape off his beard.

He made it to Wild Roots with less than a minute to spare, and his empty stomach grumbled all morning. Fortunately, Jesse didn't have time to dwell on either his hunger or last night's events. He had three appointments before noon, all friends who never returned to Shear Pleasures, delighted to have him do their hair again.

Stephanie -- who had a labret, piercings through both her eyebrows, and bracelets tattooed around her wrists -- settled into the chair and smiled at Jesse in the mirror. "So how do you like it here?"

Wrapping strands of her black hair around perm

rods, Jesse smiled. "It's just divine."

Stephanie giggled. "Seriously?"

He reached for another rod. "Seriously, I couldn't have imagined a more perfect place to work if I'd thought about it. I was just miserable at that other place, especially with no customers of my own."

"I'm sorry, Jesse. I just couldn't stand having that bitch stare at me when I walked in the door. And those other women? I swear to goddess, they're all older than my grandmother."

Jesse laughed and led Stephanie over to the dryer. "It was pretty oppressive, but one has to start somewhere." He lowered the dryer hood. "Can I get you something to drink or read?"

"Water's fine and I have my phone." Stephanie waved it at Jesse and then manipulated her thumbs across the keyboard.

He brought her a bottle of water, and cleaned up his station while she sat under the dryer. When she left, he checked his phone and found he had two messages from Tony, one voice and one text. Both instructed Jesse to come straight to Tony's house after work.

Jesse spent the rest of the day trying not to obsess about what lay ahead. On the one hand, Tony made him fly and he'd forgotten how much he needed that. But Ashleigh never expected him to service her sexually in payment. And, he resented Tony's assumption that he was available at his command.

He sighed. Ashleigh had treated him the same way and he missed her so much. She'd handed him over to Tony. If he pissed off Tony in any way before he built up his customer base, he might lose his fabulous new job.

Doting on his ladies, Jesse found just the right magazine or beverage for each and made sure their hair looked better than ever. Of course, having the right product and equipment made that easier. Still, he needed to prove himself worthy of Wild Roots. He didn't want Christopher to keep him on just for Tony's sake. Jesse even stayed late to help tidy up the salon.

Christopher found Jesse sweeping up and flicked the back of his hands in Jesse's direction. "Shoo, dear. I've a cleaning crew to do that. You've put in a lovely day, I'm quite pleased. Tomorrow we'll talk about setting up a referral program so your friends can get discounts for sending you new customers."

Jesse replaced the broom on its hook. "We could do that now, if you'd like."

Christopher laughed. "I don't know about you, darling, but I have a date." He leaned over one of the stations, checking his hair in the mirror and pulling strands into place. "Work-life balance, you know. And if I had a hot hunk like Tony to go home to at the end of the day, this shop would close an hour earlier." He winked at Jesse in the mirror.

Jesse caught site of his own reflection in the same mirror, his lips pressed together into a tight smile that looked just like his mother's. He ran the back of his hand over his lips to wipe it away. He should have known Christopher wouldn't help keep him away from Tony, especially since he apparently thought they were dating. Jesse wandered over to the bus stop, hoping he'd missed the next one, but it pulled up as he approached. The bus carried him past his own stop and Jesse wanted so much to get off, but he had no clue how to extricate himself from

Tony's expectation that he would obey his summons.

Tony lived in a one-story house in the southwest hills. A steep driveway led up to wooden stairs that rose to a front porch running the entire length of the house. A worn sofa that may have once been blue sat between the steps and the front window, a spring poking through one cushion and padding showing through the frayed armrests.

The door swung open when Jesse rang the bell, but he saw no one. He edged inside, and the door closed to reveal a man with very bleached blond hair and tattoo sleeves. He wore a steel collar and leather wrist cuffs and nothing else.

He held out a hand. "You must be Jesse. I'm Shane."

Jesse accepted the hand and tried not to stare.

"Tony's with Demon in the back room. He said to make sure you ate before I sent you back." Shane turned and headed through a doorway that led to a huge kitchen. A retro fifties, metal-edged, laminate table and six metal chairs with shiny red plastic seats and backs sat in the corner between large floor-length windows. The smell of chili permeated the kitchen, reminding Jesse that the entire day he'd only eaten half a sandwich that a co-worker shared when she figured out he hadn't brought anything for lunch.

Shane handed him a deep, black bowl with a spoon in it. "Help yourself. There's pop in the fridge and crackers on the table." He pointed to both in turn. "Don't dawdle, Tony doesn't like us to keep him waiting." Shane left Jesse alone in the kitchen.

He filled the bowl from the large stock pot on the stove and took a seat at the table. He blew on a spoonful of beans and meat for a moment inhaling the scent of peppers and cumin. Someone in the house knew how to cook. The chili satisfied his hunger, but did nothing to ease his self doubt and his uncertainty about his relationship with Tony. After polishing off his second helping of chili, he set the bowl in the sink and stepped back into the living room, trying to figure out where to find the "back." The living room had a big round coffee table and black vinyl sofas with wooden legs and arms.

Past the front entrance, he found a dark, narrow hallway with several closed doors on each side. At the end of the hall, light spilled out from the one open room, guiding him in that direction. When he reached the doorway, he saw a St. Andrew's cross and a massage table along one wall. Tony stood in front of the table. Jesse could see the feet of a man who had his ankles on Tony's shoulders. He stepped back, embarrassed, but bumped into Shane.

"Just take off your clothes, go into the room, and wait on your knees until Tony's ready for you." Shane held out one hand. "I can take your clothes for you."

Jesse could think of no way to extract himself from the situation graciously. He removed his skirt, blouse, and panties and handed them to Shane along with his purse. He stepped inside the room and dropped to his knees as instructed.

Tony pushed in and out of the other man's ass, grunting and groaning. One hand squeezed the other man's hard cock and the other twisted his balls. The man's head banged against the wall with each of Tony's sharp thrusts.

Jesse realized he was staring, so he lowered his eyes

to the floor for a moment then scanned the far wall. Whips, floggers, chains, and cuffs hung from hooks. Shelves held various other implements of torture.

When Tony finished, he kissed the other man and held him for a few minutes. Then he helped him climb down from the table and slapped his ass. The man knelt in front of Jesse and offered his hand. "Hey, Jesse, I go by Demon."

Jesse took it and tried not to think how ridiculous they looked, two naked men on their knees, shaking hands.

Demon grinned, rose, and left the room. Tony patted the massage table. "Your turn, boy."

Jesse couldn't move. The idea of Tony fucking him in the ass right after doing Demon without a condom made him nauseous. Even though Tony asked about his status, how could he know one of his concubines hadn't lied?

"C'mon, boy. It's 'bout time I introduced you to CBT. You think you flew last night." He laughed. "This will send you into the stratosphere."

Hoping that meant Tony didn't plan to fuck him, Jesse pushed himself to his feet and balanced on the edge of the table.

"You know what CBT is, boy?"

Jesse shrugged, "Cognitive Based Therapy, Computer Based Training, or Cock and Ball Torture."

Tony laughed. "And which do you think you're going to learn about tonight?"

Jesse hung his head. "Cock and ball torture," he whispered.

"Good boy." Tony grabbed Jesse's hair and kissed

him, then pulled his hair until he lay on his back on the table.

From a shelf on the opposite wall, Tony picked up a small cardboard box that he set it between Jesse's legs. One at a time, he removed plastic clothespins from the box and attached them to Jesse's scrotum. Each one made Jesse squeak in pain. He had to resist covering himself with his hands. While he could accept Tony blistering the skin of his back in exchange for the ecstasy of flying, he didn't feel comfortable with Tony torturing his privates.

When Jesse's balls bristled with clothespins, Tony went back to the shelf. This time, he returned with a miniature flogger, one not much longer than his hand. With it, he whipped Jesse's cock until he cried out.

Tony leaned over and whispered in Jesse's ear. "You're not using the pain to fly, boy." He ran his hand across the clothespins causing new stabs of torment.

Because you're hurting my cock, he wanted to say, but he could only grimace, unable to process the pain and find his way to bliss.

Tony ran a small, metal, spiked wheel the length of his cock. Jesse sobbed. Tears streamed down his face. He wondered if he could find anyone at the mall to hire him. Tony leaned over and bit his nipple. He shrieked and Tony chuckled.

"Please, Sir." Jesse gripped the table on either side of his hips. "Please, can we stop now?"

"Can't exactly stop now. The clothespins have to come off, eventually, and they'll hurt more coming off than they did going on. Process the pain, boy. Enjoy it. I'll give you a taste."

Tony removed one of the clothespins. The pain

intensified tenfold as blood flowed back into the pinched off area. Jesse couldn't even give voice to his agony and protest. He wanted more than anything else to be somewhere else, but he couldn't find his way to subspace. He had no idea how to reach the point where he could fly. Before, the pain always sent him there with almost no effort on his part.

Each clothespin Tony removed caused pain -- pain more excruciating than anything he'd ever known before. When the last one came off, Tony kissed him. Hoping he could distract the man from inflicting any more agony, Jesse threw his arms around his tormentor's neck and kissed him back. Tony reached down and stroked Jesse's bruised and battered genitals. His other hand cupped Jesse's cheek. Jesse clung to his neck, sobbing.

Tony's fingers stroked the underside of Jesse's balls and rubbed against his perineum. When he put his thumb against Jesse's asshole, Jesse pulled himself off the table and dropped to his knees. Desperate to avoid getting fucked in the ass without a condom, he reached for Tony's cock. Squeezing the shaft in one hand, he gently massaged his balls in the other and licked his glans, trying to ignore the punk taste, while Tony played with his hair.

It took forever to get Tony off. Jesse's jaws got tired and his knees ached. But the picture in his mind of Tony fucking Demon while twisting his balls made the still pinched skin on Jesse's scrotum ache. After what seemed like an hour of stroking, sucking, and licking, Tony finally grabbed Jesse's hair in both his hands and face fucked him hard until he came deep in his throat.

Jesse swallowed, grateful his torment had ended. He

didn't care about the taste. He only wanted to get out of the house and go home. Tony pulled him up by the hair and hugged him. Jesse buried his face in Tony's neck.

"You wanna spend the night here, boy?"

"Thanks. No. I'm okay." Jesse backed away. "If I don't get home tonight, I'll never make it to work on time tomorrow. I was almost late today."

Tony stared at him. Jesse stood straight and he knew that, unlike the night before, his eyes weren't glazed and he could walk a straight line. Tony kissed his forehead in dismissal and Jesse hurried from the room in search of Shane and his clothes.

Chapter Twenty

Jesse ignored Tony's phone calls the next day. He called back after dinner, when he was pretty sure Tony would be busy. After listening and re-recording his message five times, he finally chose the send option for: "Hey, Tony, I very much appreciate everything you've done for me ... but I really can't play during the week. I just don't do well at work the next morning, and after everything you went through to help me get the job, I don't want to disappoint you or Christopher. I'm off Sunday and Monday, so anytime you want me to come over Saturday or Sunday night, just let me know. Thanks much."

Even though it was only eight o'clock, Jesse turned off his phone and crawled into bed. He woke with a start when the alarm went off at six, realizing he didn't even remember falling asleep. But once he took a shower, he felt better than he had all week. After eating some cereal, he turned on his phone and discovered a missed call from Tony and a voicemail notification. The thought of listening to it at that moment, made his breakfast threaten to come back up, so he finished his coffee and got ready for work.

He forgot about the voicemail, which allowed him to enjoy his morning coloring and perming hair, chit chatting with his ladies and the other stylists. When Jesse took an appointment that brought his scheduled number of clients for the day to six, Christopher smiled and said "Excellent!" Jesse beamed. He skipped lunch so he could give Nicole an updo for a fundraiser that evening. By the end of the day, he felt faint when he realized he still hadn't listened to Tony's voicemail.

Christopher swept into his workstation, his eyes glittering. "Some of the boys and I are going over to Steelhead for a brewski. They've got one of the cutest waiters in town. We all just drool over him. Unfortunately, the poor boy is convinced he's straight. He even claims he's dating a girl." Christopher sighed and Jesse couldn't help but laugh at his exaggerations. "You want to join us?" his boss asked.

"Sure." It beat having to deal with Tony, and going out after work with one's boss could certainly be considered more important than anything Tony might have planned. "Let me just check my voicemail and see if I need to return a call."

"You can do that on the way over." Christopher locked the front door, then stepped over to the alarm by the back door. "We don't want to keep the boys waiting. Go ahead out while I set this. We'll take my car."

After Christopher locked the back door, he led Jesse to his baby blue Jetta. Jesse buckled his seatbelt and pulled out his cell phone. The message from Tony said:

"Saturday night we're going to the party at the Sanctuary. We'll pick you up at seven forty-five. Don't dress like a girl, for Pete's sake." Jesse deleted the message, grateful Tony had apparently accepted the limitation of play only on weekends. He wondered what the Sanctuary was, but he dared not ask Christopher.

He drove up High Street and pulled into the parking lot behind the brewery on Fifth. Inside, he waved to a group of guys in their late thirties to mid forties sitting at a large round table next to the restaurant's centerpiece, a red and glass English phone booth. Jesse and Christopher made their way from the back entrance, their heels clicking across the oak floor as they navigated through mahogany tables surrounded by oversize wingback and bent wood chairs.

When they'd joined the five others, Christopher announced: "Sweets, this is Jesse, my newest treasure at the shop."

Jesse blinked in surprise. He hadn't expected such high praise.

"Lester," Christopher pointed to the large hairy bald man to his left, then continued around the table. "Jeremy, Samuel, Michael, and Timothy."

Jesse shook all the proffered hands, knowing he'd never remember all their names.

Only the last man spoke. "Call me Tim."

"Started to wonder if you were going to join us or not." Lester had a schooner of amber-red beer between his very large hands.

"You know it takes longer to close up sometimes, 'specially when we've had a busy day." Christopher picked up the plastic covered menu. "I'm famished.

Did you boys order food, too?"

Tim drank from a glass of very dark liquid. "We waited." He had short, dark hair, heavy black-framed glasses, and a gold hoop in his left ear.

"But the next time the waiter came by, we were gonna order." The guy in between Tim and Lester, Jesse couldn't remember if he was Jeremy or Michael, wore a three-piece suit. Jesse wondered if he was a lawyer or a banker. No one else in Eugene dressed that way for work.

Christopher leaned in to the group. "Did you get Gene to wait on us?"

"Of course." Tim smiled, revealing teeth badly in need of a dentist's attention.

"He's wearing the most darling shorts." Samuel had on a tank top that showed off his chiseled muscles and a dark, very un-Oregonian tan. "Magnificent legs."

In unison, all eyes at the table turned at that moment to watch a tall, lean, dark-haired man approach. He had a goatee and mustache along with jet black eyes. Holding up an order pad, he looked at Christopher. "Can I get you two anything to drink?"

"I'll have the Steelhead pinot gris." Christopher set down the menu. "And I think we're all ready to order food now, too. You can bring me the Chinese chicken salad."

Fortunately, Gene turned to Lester next, giving Jesse time to study the menu. It was little pricier than he'd hoped. The sandwiches didn't even include potatoes. He thought about just ordering a starter, but then he discovered the chicken strips came with fries and slaw for only nine dollars. With the tips he had made, he could afford that, so when Gene turned to him, Jesse ordered and asked for a glass of water to drink.

Christopher put a hand on Gene's arm to keep him from heading back to the bar. "Nonsense, my dear. You put in an awesome day, order a drink on me."

Jesse hesitated, but Christopher said to Gene: "Put anything he wants to drink on my tab. I need to run to the little boy's room."

Jesse ordered a glass of Steelhead draft rootbeer, then studied his companions. Nothing in the men's appearance, speech, or dress seemed similar. Apparently their only commonality was their sexuality, their similar age, their love of gossip and the fact that they all thought Gene was hot. He couldn't keep up with the conversation around the table. He had no idea who they were talking about most of the time, and after a while he wasn't even sure if they spoke of real people or just the characters on television shows.

When Gene handed him his rootbeer, Jesse tried to decide what made the waiter so hot. Sure, he had a nice build and obviously worked out, but then so did Samuel. Gene's face had a youthful look that his goatee did little to age. Still, Jesse could see nothing worth the attention Gene commanded every time he approached their table.

The rootbeer had a strong sassafras flavor without being too sweet. After his third sip, Jesse decided it was probably the best, most intense rootbeer he'd ever tasted. The chicken strips definitely filled the empty hole in his stomach -- perfectly crispy skin covering moist meat. The restaurant had its merits, Jesse thought, even if he didn't think the waiter was one of them. But, as soon as he finished his meal, he placed a ten-spot on the table, added a few coins from his pocket, and leaned over to Christopher. "Thanks so much for the rootbeer, but I need to get going." Jesse stood. "Nice meeting you all."

"But, hun, I was gonna give you a ride home." Christopher looked at his friends and then at Jesse.

"Not a problem." Jesse extracted his transit pass from his bag. "I can catch the bus. I'll see you tomorrow."

Christopher gave him a wave of dismissal and turned back to his conversation. Jesse walked out of the restaurant slowly, trying to not show how eager he was to leave. "Note to self," he whispered when the door closed behind him. "Turn down all future after-work invitations from boss to avoid succumbing to terminal boredom."

Once he figured out where to catch the bus, Jesse reflected on his attitude toward the older men in the restaurant. He had to remember that they came out in times very different than his own. Although Oregon had passed the amendment to prevent same-sex marriage, the new legislature made civil unions legal. As a teen, he got more flack for his femininity than for being gay. At their age, gay men probably had to bond or end up friendless.

He thought about the collection of folks who gathered together for fetish events and S&M parties. They probably had less in common than the men sitting at the table in the Steelhead. They ranged in age from eighteen to eighty and fell into every sexual orientation imaginable. The only thing many of them shared was the pleasure they got from receiving or delivering pain.

When the bus arrived, Jesse climbed aboard, promising himself to work at being less judgmental of others.

Chapter Twenty-One

J esse rummaged through his closet, looking for something suitably "manly" to wear. He wished he had a clue what kind of place the Sanctuary was or what sort of event Tony was taking him to. He'd looked online, but hadn't found any information, and Tony hadn't updated his MySpace page in weeks. Finally, he settled on a pair of women's blue jeans and a black blouse made of shiny polyester with a simple cut and a breast pocket. He rolled up the long sleeves to hide the three-button cuffs and pulled his hair into a ponytail.

Tony arrived in a rusty black Plymouth van with Shane in the front seat and Demon in the back. Jesse climbed in behind Shane and Tony took off. They drove through an industrial area of town and pulled into a warehouse parking lot. Tony turned off the engine and Shane jumped out to grab a large plastic tub from the back. Demon opened Tony's door. Jesse followed the three across the street and up the driveway of what looked like a fire station. They led him to a single door next to the large, closed, overhead door and he followed them inside.

Tony, Demon, and Shane pulled out plastic cards and offered them -- along with ten dollar bills -- to the blonde woman behind a desk. Tony pointed his thumb at Jesse. "He'll have to join. I've vouched for him."

The woman wore a brocade corset that pushed her breasts up almost to her chin. She handed Tony a ballpoint pen and several sheets of paper on a clipboard. She pointed to a series of church pews that lined two walls of the room. "You can fill them out over there."

Jesse sat down and read the list of rules. The one recommending safer sex and urging the use of "supplies to protect against any kind of fluid exchange" made him wonder what Tony had planned for the evening. When he got to the waiver sheet, he wondered if he could get away with refusing to initial next to the item that said: "In consideration of the right to participate in consensual bondage and/or sadomasochistic activities (BDSM), or the viewing of these and any other activities in which I may participate, I hereby certify that I am in good physical, mental, emotional, and psychological health." He closed his eyes and tried to figure out someway to escape. Nothing came to him, and he knew Tony wouldn't appreciate his claim of mental health issues. He signed both forms.

On the membership application, he'd no idea what to put for "scene name," so he just put "Jesse." He had no clue what to choose on the line with check boxes beside top, bottom, dom, sub, switch, so he marked "other."

The sexuality line was easy, although he wondered how one could be "other" than heterosexual, gay, lesbian, or bisexual. He checked "gay." Then he got to "relationship status." He wanted to check single, but he didn't think Tony would find that acceptable. That left "partnered," "poly," or "other." Once again, he opted for "other" not knowing what else applied. Hell, he still didn't know what "poly" meant. He answered the rest of the questions and offered the papers back to the blonde, who asked for his identification and twenty dollars.

Jesse sighed. "How often do you have parties here?"

She filled out a membership card with "Jesse" on it, put it between two pieces of plastic, and stuck it in a laminator. "Last Saturday of every month. You only have to pay membership once a year, and if you bring a potluck contribution, it only costs you five dollars to get in." She handed him the still warm card, now encased in plastic. "Just be sure to bring that with you."

At least he wouldn't be expected to shell out twenty dollars every weekend. Jesse stuck the card in his wallet and put it in the front pocket of his jeans. "Thanks."

The blonde came around from behind the desk and a six-foot tall man wearing a blue tulle gown with a handkerchief hem took her place. Jesse wondered why Tony had insisted he wear something "manly." The blonde waved an arm. "I'll give you a tour, now. This is the social area." She stepped around a partial wall that blocked the entrance from the rest of the room and pointed to a glass wall. "That's the main dungeon."

Jesse stared through the glass at the huge cement block room on the other side of the large overhead door he'd seen from outside. Padded tables, St. Andrew's crosses, and a large metal cage lined three walls. A wooden contraption in the center resembled a jungle gym, and on the far wall, alcoves held two gilt thrones and a door which led into another room.

The blonde touched Jesse's arm, and he roused himself enough to follow her along a dark, narrow hallway past a room with a sign that said "Private" taped on the closed door. "Bathroom." They passed an open door and he could see a double sink, toilet, and shower. She pointed to a closed door past the bathroom. "You can use this room for toybags IF the storage room off the kitchen is full." They continued down the hallway. At the far end, a door to the right revealed a room with an exam table, medical cabinets, and various other equipment. "Medical scene room. Only place blood play's allowed." She turned and pointed to the area opposite with a wall of lockers and two old fashioned school desks. "For classroom scenes."

The blonde stepped through the doorway at the end of the hall. "This is the Japanese bondage room." The room had bamboo floors and a kimono displayed on the wall. A padded table, a rope rack, and another St. Andrew's cross were arranged against the walls, along with a blowup bed that had cuffs attached to the four corners. "Please remove your shoes before entering this room and keep all food and beverages out of here."

The blonde moved back down the hall, and Jesse stepped aside to let her pass. After they cleared the classroom, she opened a door on the right and led him through the far end of the main dungeon to the door next to the two thrones. "This is the kitchen, also used as a social area."

Jesse stepped in to find the room crowded with

people wearing fetish gear, simple black, or nothing at all. Many held paper plates filled with food. Along the far walls, two tables covered with plastic stood at right angles to each other. The food offerings reminded him of the parties at Lady Nell's and Randy's houses, the ones Ashleigh and Rachel took him to. On the counter next to the sink, a large coffee pot percolated and bottles of water and juice filled a cooler under one of the tables.

The blonde pointed to the door straight ahead. "Outdoor smoking area." She showed him a small room off the hall between the dungeon and the door leading outside. "You can stash your toybag and clothing in here." One wall had small metal lockers. Suitcases and duffle bags covered the floor, and a couple of long tubes leaned upright in the corners. "Any questions?"

Jesse shook his head.

"Have fun. I need to get back to the desk."

Jesse wondered what he should do next. Ashleigh had always played with Rachel first, so he could eat. He had no idea where Tony and his boys had disappeared to or what was expected of him. Peeking through the glass in the top of the door between the kitchen and the dungeon, he saw women bound to either side of the jungle gym and Tony chaining Demon up to one of the crosses. Apparently, he wouldn't be required for a while. He found a plate and filled it with food.

A woman who towered over him reached for a cookie from a clamshell container on the table. "First time here?" She wore a black leather corset dress that cinched her waist and showed off impressive breasts. Some of her height came from the platform heels she wore, but even without those, Jesse guessed she was his height.

"Yes, Ma'am." Jesse took a plastic fork from a cup on a shelf above the table hoping to avoid unwanted attention by stuffing potato salad in his mouth.

She nibbled on the cookie and looked at him. He felt like a piece of meat on display in the grocery store. "You looking to play?"

"Ma'am?" Jesse mumbled around the dill and onion flavors in his mouth, holding one hand in front of his lips. He had the overwhelming feeling that he should only speak to this woman from his knees.

"Would you like to bottom to me?"

Jesse wanted to say yes, but that didn't seem appropriate. "I'm sorry, but I came with someone. I expect he'll want to play with me."

"You only do one scene a night?" She licked cookie crumbs off her lips, and Jesse found his eyes mesmerized by her tongue.

"Ma'am?"

"Is this your first party, boy?"

"No, Ma'am. I've been to house parties before." Jesse stuffed more food into his mouth without tasting it, trying to avoid her piercing stare.

"Can you only manage one scene a night? Do you know what your friend plans to do? I could do something else, if you're interested."

Jesse pondered her suggestion. He had no clue what Tony planned for him, but the idea of letting this stunning woman send him flying had a lot of appeal.

"Normally, he flogs and single tails me. Sometimes he does CBT." Jesse found himself wondering what it'd be like to have this woman abuse his cock, and if he'd like it more than when Tony did it.

"We just met, so I think I'll pass on the CBT." She brushed off her hands and offered him her right one. "I'm Mistress Dianne."

He shook her hand. "Jesse."

"Do you like electrical play?"

Jesse shrugged. "What's that?"

She laughed. "How adventurous are you?"

"Not very."

"What about caning?"

Ashleigh had caned him several times. He had trouble sitting down for several days, but it did send him flying. "Sure."

She smiled and walked over to the storage room. "Grab that cane bag, boy." She pointed to one of the black tubes. "The one in the far corner."

Jesse stepped over the various bags until he could reach the case she wanted. He followed her through the dungeon and down the hall to the Japanese room. She stuck her head inside, then stepped out of her shoes, which made her just slightly shorter than he. Even without the shoes, though, she still carried herself in a way that made her seem taller. Jesse used his toes to push off his loafers and handed her the cane bag. She extracted several long rods -- one acrylic, one rattan, one maple, and one fiberglass -- laid them across the padded table and looked at Jesse. "These all okay?"

He shrugged. He had no idea what the question meant. He unbuttoned his shirt and removed it, hanging it from the back of a chair against the wall. He folded his jeans and set them on the seat with his panties tucked inside.

She picked up the canes and lay all but the rattan one

on top of his jeans. He climbed up on the table and lay on his stomach. Mistress Dianne leaned over with her mouth near his ear, her hot breath blowing across it. "Do you need a long, slow warm up?"

"No, Ma'am." With his head resting on his forearms, he could see the canes arrayed across the denim and his butt quivered in anticipation.

"You a heavy bottom?"

Jesse puzzled over that question. He thought his ass fairly attractive, not heavy at all.

"Do you like to play hard, boy?"

"Yes, Ma'am."

She ran one hand down his back and across his butt and Jesse trembled. "Any medical conditions I should know about?"

"No, Ma'am."

"You ready, boy?" she whispered in his ear.

"Yes, Ma'am."

She struck his ass lightly with the cane, slowly at first, then steadily increasing both her speed and the weight of her strokes. His ass was just starting to feel warm when she switched to the maple cane. The blows became stingier and Jesse let the pain invade his mind. By the time she picked up the acrylic cane, he was flying. She ran her hand across his ass and he reveled in the feel of soft skin of her hand against his emerging welts.

"How you doing, boy?"

Jesse smiled.

She slid her fingers into his hair and picked his head up off the table. "I need a verbal answer, boy. You want me to keep going?"

"Please, Ma'am." Jesse wondered why she was asking

him, but he didn't care as long as she continued caning him. Euphoria overwhelmed him, and he floated into the agony and ecstasy of pain.

Jesse had no idea when or if Mistress Dianne switched to the fiberglass cane, or exactly when she stopped beating his butt. He only knew that eventually she'd wrapped him in a blanket and held him in her arms and that his face nestled within licking distance of those impressive breasts. He attributed his desire to stick out his tongue and taste them to the euphoria fogging his brain and floated in the bliss.

Chapter Twenty-Two

"**W**hat the HELL is going on here?"

"Aftercare." Lady Dianne's voice seemed further away than physically possible.

"For what?" Tony's seemed entirely too close. "Who gave you permission to play with this boy in the first place?"

"Excuse me. Exactly who do you think you're talking to? I don't see a collar around this boy's neck. He and I negotiated a scene that didn't include you as a participant in any way, shape or form." Lady Dianne hugged Jesse protectively closer and he wrapped his arms around her waist. He wondered if she was a lesbian, and if she'd take care of him like Ashleigh had.

Rough fingers in Jesse's hair yanked his head back, and he found himself staring up into Tony's eyes. "Who the fuck gave you permission to play with anyone else, boy? Especially a female?"

Jerked out of subspace, Jesse responded carefully.

"I'm sorry, Sir, I didn't know I required your permission to play with anyone. You were busy with Demon, and the Lady Dianne made me a most enticing offer." The grip on Jesse's hair relaxed a little, but Tony didn't release him. "She only caned my ass, so the rest of my body is available for your pleasure, Sir." Jesse wanted to puke on his own words, but he also didn't want Tony angry at him. What if Tony convinced Christopher to fire him?

Tony let go of Jesse's hair and stood up. "I'll play with any part of your body I choose, including your ass if I wish. And I'm ready now. Shane's holding a cross in the main dungeon. Don't keep me waiting."

Turning on his heel, Tony stomped out of the bondage room.

"Boy, you don't have to put up with that kind of abuse."

Lady Dianne stroked his hair, and he wanted nothing more than to stay in her arms, to recapture the bubble of euphoria Tony had burst. But he knew better. "Thank you, Ma'am, I'll be fine." Jesse pulled away, and Lady Dianne opened her arms to let him go. He pushed himself to his feet. "Thank you, Ma'am, for a most excellent scene. I'm so very sorry we were interrupted in the end, but I enjoyed it immensely. I hope you did, too."

Lady Dianne frowned. She rose to her feet and took a container of bleach wipes from a small table in the corner. "You'd better go boy, you don't want to keep your *Master* waiting." She pulled out one of the wipes and used it to clean her canes.

Jesse knew he should stay and help her clean up, but he feared further angering Tony. He grabbed his clothes and headed out of the room, stopping only to pick up his shoes.

Inside the main dungeon, every station except one was in use. Naked males and females accepted pain from those who wielded whips, canes, clamps, candle flames, knives, and other nasty things. Tony stood next to the one empty cross at the far side of the dungeon, his arms crossed over his bare chest. Jesse hurried over to his side and knelt in front of him.

"That's better, boy." Tony patted his head. "Go stick your clothes in a locker and come back here. Bring a bottle of water."

"Yes, Sir." Jesse scurried back to the kitchen, found an empty locker for his clothing, and grabbed a bottle of water from the cooler.

When Jesse handed him the bottle, Tony swallowed a long swig, then pointed to the cross. Jesse stood facing it and Tony ran his hand across Jesse's butt. "Wow, she really did a number on your ass. You'd better turn around."

Jesse did as he was told. Tony buckled his wrists and ankles into leather cuffs and attached them to the cross. He pulled his signal whip from the plastic bin and stepped back. Tony cracked the whip and hit Jesse's left nipple. Jesse cried out in pain. When Tony hit the other one, Jesse shrieked.

Tony stepped in closer. "I thought you'd be all warmed up from the bitch you decided to play with first."

Before Jesse could respond, Tony stepped back and threw again, this time with much less force. But, the whip kissed the tip of Jesse's cock. He had to bite his tongue to keep from screaming. Tony continued snapping the whip at him, hitting his nipples, his cock, his balls, the inside of his thighs, and his armpits. Tears flowed down Jesse's face and he just wanted the agony to end. He tried to find his way back into subspace, but the pain had gotten too intense too quickly.

By the time Tony stopped, Jesse hung from the cuffs, his fingers numb, and the rest of his body in excruciating agony. Tony snapped his fingers at Shane. "Take care of him," he said and walked away.

Shane removed the cuffs that held Jesse to the cross and took his weight, helping him to the ground. He covered Jesse with a blanket and handed him the half empty water bottle Tony had left behind. Jesse tried to open it, but his fingers wouldn't work. The bottle ended up back on the floor. Shane removed the cap and held it to Jesse's lips so he could gulp it down.

Then Shane took Jesse's cock in his fingers and moved it around so he could examine it. "I'd better get you some ice for that. Hang on, I'll be right back."

Jesse didn't think he liked the idea of putting ice on his penis, but he also feared continuation of the horrid pain and would welcome any relief.

Shane returned with a handful of ice in a paper cup and set it on the floor in front of Jesse. He scooped out about half, gently put Jesse's cock in the cup and piled ice on top of it. The cold hurt, but not as much as the red welts Tony had left with his whip.

"Thanks."

Shane took his chin in his fingers and turned Jesse's head from one side to the other. "I'd a been flying if Tony played with me like that. What'sup?"

Jesse shrugged. "I played with someone else. He

thought I was warmed up, but I totally lost subspace when he interrupted the aftercare." The cold on his cock seemed to intensify the pain and Jesse wanted to pull out, but common sense told him cold now would mean less pain later. "He's a bit upset with me."

"Why, he doesn't care if we play with other guys, s'long as we ask first." Shane held the water bottle up again for Jesse to finish.

"I didn't ask and it wasn't a guy." Jesse swallowed the rest of the water.

Shane grimaced. "Dude, why in the world'd you wanna to play with a dame?"

Jesse shrugged. "My friend Ashleigh introduced me to S&M, and for that matter, to Tony. I just let Lady Dianne cane me, it's not like I had sex with her."

"You played with Lady D?" Shane's eyes widened. "I suggest you stay away from her in the future if you don't want Tony really pissed at you."

Jesse pulled the blanket tighter around himself. The ice on his cock made him shiver with cold. "Why?"

"Let's just say that she and Tony don't get along, and you'd do better keeping your distance from her as long as you're in service to Tony."

Jesse wanted to ask what the hell Shane meant by "in service to Tony," but Shane left to get something to clean the cross with. By the time he returned, the pain had evened up enough for Jesse to find his way back to subspace and he floated oblivious to Shane and everyone else in the dungeon.

Chapter Twenty-Three

After almost six hours in the van, they finally turned onto a dirt road that dipped down into the trees. A sign warned that they'd entered a religious sanctuary. Jesse stared at Demon, puzzled. "I thought you were all atheists?"

"Not that kind of religion, Dude."

The van pulled up next to a kiosk alongside the road. Everyone clambered out. They signed waivers, produced ID, and handed over credit cards. Jesse whistled when he saw the amount on the slip he signed.

"I still can't believe we're paying a hundred and thirty five bucks each to camp out for three nights."

"That includes three squares, boy." Tony stuffed his wallet back into one of the pouches on his kilt.

"And, there's a pool and two hot tubs." The girl who'd checked his identification had bright blue eyes that sparkled in the late afternoon sun. She fastened a plastic purple band around his wrist.

Jesse raised his hands, palm up. "Okay, whatever. It

still empties out my savings account."

"Hey, Dude! This is Paradise! Lighten up." Demon draped an arm over Jesse's shoulder. "I promise, when we head home on Monday you'll start counting the days until you can come back."

Jesse doubted that. He found the idea of spending Labor Day weekend camping in the wilds of Washington distasteful. He preferred his own bed, hot showers, and other comforts of home. But Tony insisted coming here would change his life and after a couple of months as one of Tony's toys, Jesse needed some kind of change. He just had no clue what.

They piled back into the van and followed the narrow dirt road down the hill until they found a parking space in the area behind a small berm, between a stone circle and a long, log house.

"Okay, let's get everything unloaded so we can get the car out of the way." Tony opened the back hatch and grabbed one of the dozen or so large, covered plastic bins. Jesse clutched another one to his chest and followed him past a small stucco house out into an open meadow filled with tents of every shape, size and color. Tony wound his way through, occasionally greeting someone they knew. By the time they reached an open area big enough to satisfy Tony, Jesse guessed half the Eugene S&M community had beaten them up here.

Tony had each of them put their bins in four corners of the space he wanted to stake out before he sent them back to the van for more. When Jesse returned to the campsite, he saw a tall, stocky, bald fellow with studs in both ears stroll past. He was leading someone in a pink pig costume by a leash attached to its collar. Jesse dropped his load and stared. The pig's head had tiny pink ears, a big snout, and big black eyes. He wondered how whoever was inside could see.

Tony dropped the tent and poles in the middle of the space with a clatter. "No time to gawk, boy. Want to get camp set up 'fore dinner."

"Yes, Sir." Jesse headed back to the car, but everywhere he looked, he found something to stare at. He spotted a man, naked except for chains and leather straps, hooked up to a pony cart. He wore a leather harness around his head, attached to a blindfold. A leather snout with two air holes in it suck out from his face. A woman wearing a leather corset dress and knee-high boots sat in the cart, flicking a whip at the man pulling it.

Jesse shook his head and returned to the car for another load. When they'd moved everything to their space, Shane drove the van away and they unfolded the tent to set it up. Jesse heard the slap of leather on skin, keeping time with the hammer that pounded the stakes in the ground although he couldn't see who was playing. They'd just finished raising the tent when they heard the clang of metal on metal.

Tony looked at his watch. "We're third shift, so we've got an hour to finish setting up camp." They stashed everything in the tent, organizing it to meet Tony's standards, and draped a rain fly over the top. Finally, Tony allowed them to use the toilets at the edge of the campgrounds. When they returned to the tent, Tony handed them each a metal plate and cup and a set of tableware. "Let's go eat."

Jesse followed the three men across the circle of standing stones to join the line that formed behind an open air kitchen. The aroma of spicy barbecued chicken and baked beans made Jesse salivate. They'd left Eugene later than planned and Tony had refused to stop for food.

Four people wielded serving utensils from behind pots and pans on the other side of the counter. In the middle of the road passing the kitchen stood a black trough on a metal stand which held potato salad, an assortment of chopped vegetables, salad dressing, and other condiments. A tall, bearded fellow wearing a white apron over his tee shirt and kilt held a giant pair of tongs. "Would you like a piece of chicken?"

"Yes, please." Jesse extended the plate and licked his lips when he saw the large breast that the man gave him. As he made his way along the counter, a skewer of roasted vegetables and a generous spoonful of beans joined the chicken. He opted to put the strawberry shortcake in his coffee cup. From the trough, he added some potato salad, but he really had no room for anything else. At least he apparently didn't have to worry about going hungry this weekend.

Around the corner, rows of picnic tables stood under white canopies in front of a stage. The four of them found seats at one and dug into their food. Three naked women walked past the tables, waving their hands about as they talked. Jesse took his eyes away from the panorama only long enough to scoop up food. A man and woman walked by holding hands. Neither of them had any clothing on, either.

The folks at the tables around them all wore at least a sarong, although many were only clothed from the waist down. Jesse seemed to recall something from one of the papers he signed about covering one's ass during meals.

He hoped Tony wouldn't require him to wander around naked. He'd gotten less self conscious about stripping to scene in front of others, but he didn't think he could handle walking around this huge place with everything swinging free.

He cleaned his plate, but didn't taste the rest of his dinner. The spectacle of folks wandering past the dining area provided too much of a distraction. Some folks dressed in leather. others in vinyl. He counted at least five male-to-female cross dressers and three female-to-male, although he couldn't be sure about a few others. Several folks wore full pirate regalia and many sported leather and metal cuffs, collars, and leashes.

When they crossed back across the stone circle, Jesse saw a table covered with a white cloth, set with flickering candles. The fellow he'd seen earlier leading the pig around sat there with a woman in a strapless, sparkly black evening gown. A waiter wearing a tuxedo with a white napkin over his arm served them from a tray, with all the incongruity of a mustard commercial.

Jesse ran to catch up with Tony, only to follow him back to the stone circle after he grabbed a bin of toys from the tent. Near the couple at the cloth-covered table, he dropped the bin with a clatter of metal in front of the tallest standing stone. Jesse watched the couple eating and talking as if they sat in an elegant restaurant, until Tony snapped his fingers at him. He obediently stripped out of his jeans and tee shirt. By the time he'd removed his clothing, Tony had pulled several lengths of chain from the bin. In minutes, he had the chain wrapped around the rock. He locked Jesse to it with steel bracelets.

Tony warmed Jesse up with a buffalo hide flogger,

then lashed him with a six-foot bullwhip, occasionally cracking it near Jesse's ear to make him jump. Jesse let the pain envelop him and send him flying. When Tony had covered Jesse's back with enough welts to send him sailing into euphoria, he removed the cuffs, grabbed Jesse's hair, kissed him, and pulled him down to his knees. Jesse put his head under Tony's kilt and took his cock in his mouth, deep throating it and pushing his lips against Tony's pubic hair. Jesse had gotten to the point where, as long as he was in subspace, he could suck cock all night long. He didn't even mind swallowing, although he still hated taking it in the ass. Fortunately, Tony usually preferred Demon or Shane for that. Jesse still insisted on condoms and Tony liked to bareback.

When Tony shot his load, he had Demon take Jesse back to the tent while he chained Shane to the rock. Demon walked with one arm under Jesse's shoulder, then tucked him into his sleeping bag. Jesse curled up on his side, stoned. Demon kissed him, licking Tony's taste from his lips. When Demon left, Jesse listened to the sounds of leather and wood on flesh, screams of pain and passion, and raucous laughter.

Chapter Twenty-Four

Jesse woke in time to make it to the kitchen for breakfast, unlike anyone else in Tony's tent. He took one each of the three flavors of muffins from pans on the counter, then found toaster waffles at the other end and added one of those to his plate as well. He looked around for coffee. He could smell it, but was too groggy to figure out where.

A tall, slender woman wearing a black camisole, denim shorts, and Teva sandals stood at the counter, sprinkling raisins over a glob of oatmeal on her plate. "Whatcha need, hun?" A large butterfly clip held her long auburn hair on the top of her head and sunglasses prevented him from seeing her eyes.

"Coffee?"

"Hang on, I'll show you." She picked up her empty cup. "I take it you joined us yesterday?" She smiled, revealing teeth the color of pearls. Jesse just stared until she walked away.

He got his wits together enough to follow her toward

the dining area. She stopped on the way and ducked into a white canvas tent. There he found the two giant coffee urns that produced the aroma. In addition to the coffee, a selection of snacks and tea bags covered the table. Following her lead, he filled his cup then added sugar and powdered creamer.

When the woman walked outside and sat at one of the tables, Jesse seated himself across from her. He realized he'd assumed she wouldn't mind. "Is it okay if I join you?" He didn't put his plate and cup down until she nodded. "My friends are still sleeping." He wanted to hit himself, that made it sound like he only wanted to sit with her because he didn't have anyone else to talk to.

She smiled, and Jesse tried to relax. "Where you from?"

"Eugene, Oregon." He sipped his coffee, trying to find alertness in the bitter brew. He quickly took a bite of muffin to help make it palatable. Although the food all tasted great so far, the coffee wasn't in the same league.

"You know Randy?"

Jesse smiled. "Everyone in the Eugene community knows Randy."

"He introduced me to the scene, years ago when I attended U of O." She sipped her coffee. "What's your name?"

"Jesse, Ma'am." If he sipped the coffee after a bite of muffin or waffle, it was tolerable.

"I'm Lady Tina." She held out her hand, palm facing down.

Jesse brought his palm up under hers and lowered his lips to her hand, not daring to bring them close enough to touch her fingers. "Very pleased to meet you, Ma'am.

May I ask where you live now?"

"Seattle." She took a spoonful of oatmeal, never taking her eyes off Jesse. "I'm teaching a class on CBT this afternoon. Would you like to be my demo bottom?"

Jesse dropped his fork. "Ma'am?" When Ashleigh'd decided Jesse needed to try cock and ball torture, she'd turned him over to Tony. Although willing to whip, paddle, and stick needles in him, Ashleigh had drawn the line at handling his genitals.

"Have you ever done CBT?"

"Yes, Ma'am, I've had a fair amount of experience in that area." Jesse stuffed his mouth full of syrup-covered waffle, trying to buy time.

"Perfect. What are your limits?"

"I'm not permitted to have limits, Ma'am."

Lady Tina cocked her head to one side. Jesse found the resulting expression utterly charming. "I'm sorry, you're not wearing a collar, I thought you were unowned. Too bad. You're kind of cute."

Jesse tried to process a myriad reactions to her statements. "I'm not owned, Ma'am." Tony had never claimed him, never put a collar on him, even though both Demon and Shane wore one. Still, most of the folks in Eugene considered him one of Tony's boys. He expected Jesse to be available to play whenever he wanted, usually once or twice a weekend. Sometimes that play ended in sex, sometimes it didn't. As long as Tony made him fly, Jesse didn't care about anything else.

"Then who doesn't permit you to have limits?"

Jesse had to think about that. He'd no idea how Tony would want to be identified in their relationship. "It's complicated." He couldn't think of a better answer.

"You allowed to play with others?"

Jesse found it interesting that she assumed he'd want to play with her. He should tell her that he was gay, except he did want her to play with him. "Sometimes. I can ask."

She looked at her watch. "My class starts at twelve-thirty. My demo bottom blew out his clutch and hasn't made it up from the peninsula. Need to know if you're available fairly soon or I should ask someone else."

"If Ma'am can wait here for fifteen minutes, I'll be right back." Jesse left his plate and cup on the table and darted back toward the tent. He hoped Tony wasn't still asleep. He wasn't likely to give permission for anything if Jesse woke him.

When he arrived at the tent, he could hear Tony fucking, presumably Shane since he could see Demon practicing kata in front of the small cement shrine at one end of the camping area. *Great.* The only thing Tony hated worse than someone waking him prematurely was someone interrupting sex. Jesse knelt outside the tent, listening to the noises inside. Tony growled and Jesse could hear him slamming against Shane's butt. Five minutes later, they emerged from the tent.

"Would you like me to get you some breakfast, Sir?" Shane asked.

Tony nodded, and Shane grabbed plates from the tent and dashed off for the kitchen.

"Sir, a lady giving a workshop on CBT asked me if I'd demo bottom for her this afternoon. Apparently the man who had promised to bottom for her had car trouble and couldn't make it."

"She know you don't get hard when someone tortures

your junk?" Tony played with Jesse's hair. "Some folk don't like playing with a boneless package."

"I don't think she cares, Sir. I will ask her and make sure, though."

"What time's her class?" Tony sat in the single camp chair they'd brought.

"Twelve-thirty."

"Okay." Tony took the plate and cup that Shane, panting, brought back, sipped the coffee and grimaced. "This stuff's horrible."

"There's an espresso bar set up over by the house, Sir. I'll purchase you something more to your liking." Shane went in the tent, emerged with his wallet, and dashed off again.

Tony looked at Jesse. "Just be sure you find me right after class. I wanna play with you and there's a comedy show tonight after dinner I wanna see."

"Yes, Sir. Thank you, Sir." Jesse ran back, delighted to find Lady Tina still sitting at the table. Another woman sat next to her, a full-bodied blonde wearing a blue and purple sarong tied under her amble breasts. Jesse stood panting from his mad sprint.

"Good grief, boy, where'd you have to run for permission, Seattle?" Lady Tina waved at the bench across from herself. "Sit down and catch your breath."

Jesse complied and Lady Tina turned back to the blonde. "Of course, I'd love to play with you, Lisbeth. I'm available after my class. How about three o'clock?"

"Thank you, Ma'am. Shall I meet you there?"

Lady Tina nodded. "I'm teaching in the yurt classroom. See you then."

Jesse smiled. If Lady Tina was a lesbian, that'd

explain why she wanted a gay boy for her demo bottom. "Ma'am, I got permission to demo bottom for you, but was instructed to let you know I'm usually flaccid during CBT," Jesse felt heat rising to his cheeks, "and make sure this wouldn't present a problem for you."

Lady Tina smiled and Jesse thought her most beautiful. "Not a problem, boy. Be at the yurt no later than twelve-fifteen." She pointed to the purple band around his wrist. "You're not supposed to eat lunch 'til noon. Just show up at eleven and tell them you're my demo bottom."

Jesse noticed her arm band was blue. "Is that what this color means?" He thought they'd gotten purple because they were gay.

"They stagger mealtimes, except for breakfast, to keep the crowds down in front of the kitchen." She picked up her arm. "Speakers and volunteers get blue, so we don't miss meals."

She stood, picking up her plate and cup. "Since this is your first year here, feel free to ask questions. I've attended since it started seven years ago."

"Thank you, Ma'am." Jesse reached toward her plate. "May I wash your dishes for you?"

Lady Tina rewarded him with another of her brilliant smiles and set her dishes on top of his. "Thanks, boy. I need to check in with the volunteer staff." She pointed to a round, screen tent set up across from the one housing coffee. "Bring them to me there."

When Jesse returned her clean dishes, Lady Tina headed off in the opposite direction of where he camped with Tony. Since no one had any use for him until after lunch, Jesse decided to explore. He didn't want Lady

Tina to think he was following her, so he went behind the volunteer tent where he found a giant bonfire surrounded by chairs. Most of the people sitting in the chairs were smoking, so Jesse skirted the area. He saw more tents off to the right and was curious about how many folk attended. Straight ahead he saw an outdoor hot tub sunk in a large wooden deck that looked out over wetlands.

Three naked woman and two naked men soaked in the tub. Jesse wondered if he could join them. *Why not?* He stripped out of his shorts and tee shirt and set them on one of the metal chairs scattered across the deck. He saw a sign instructing folks to shower before entering the tub. At one end of the deck, he found a faucet connected to a pipe with a shower head at the top. Keeping his back to the hot tub, and the people in it, Jesse stood under it and rinsed himself off in the warm water.

When he climbed into the tub, one of the women greeted him. "Hi, I'm Noreen, this is Dick, Sir James, Baby Girl, and Raptor." She pointed to each of the occupants in turn.

Jesse feared he wouldn't remember the names, so he repeated them to himself several times. "I'm Jesse from Eugene. This is my first time here."

Noreen laughed. "Me too. Isn't it grand?"

Jesse shrugged. "Just got here last night, so I'm not really sure what it's all about."

Raptor stood up, put her rear on the edge of the tub, and boosted herself onto the lip, letting her feet dangle in the water. "Transformation. Discover who you are deep down inside, and find the acceptance to be that person." She had cropped short hair except for a long braided tail that hung down her back. A two-inch bright red streak cut through the blond. On one bicep she had the tattoo of a wolf. An inked snake wrapped around her other.

"This is sacred space dedicated to spiritual freedom." Raptor had one hand on either side of her slender hips and Jesse tried not to look at either her small breasts or the curly blond hair between her legs. "Whatever you hide from the rest of the world, you can reveal here."

If that was the case, Jesse wondered why Tony had wanted him to bring only one sundress for the entire weekend. He shrugged, he had a shawl that he sometimes wore with the sundress. Maybe he could wrap that around his waist as a skirt before he went to lunch. After all, neither Lady Tina nor Tony would need him clothed for long.

"Most of us don't live in a town as accepting as Eugene." Noreen lifted her arms out of the water and rested them on the lip of the tub. The movement brought her breasts above the water long enough for Jesse to see she had both nipples pierced with barbells. "So we have to hide who we are when we go to work and often from our families. Here we get to stay true to ourselves for an entire week." She touched the lock that hung from a thick chain around her neck.

Jesse smiled. "Not all of Eugene's that accepting. I took plenty of grief in high school and college. That's partly why I decided not to go to U.O. even though I had a scholarship."

Baby Girl stood up and opened her arms. "Hug?"

Jesse opened his eyes wide and stared. She had beautiful melon-sized breasts, firm and ripe with bright pink areola.

After a moment, she put her arms down. "It's okay. Not everyone's touchy feely. Lots of folks are, but everyone knows to ask permission."

Part of Jesse regretted the missed opportunity and part wondered what he'd have done if Baby Girl had followed through on her offer. He noticed movement in the water where Sir James sat and realized Noreen was foot fucking him. The man sat with his head leaning back against the edge of the tub, his eyes closed and a smile on his face.

"Aren't there limitations?" Jesse wondered if the man intended to spurt in the pool and whether he'd take offense if Jesse climbed out first.

"Just what's in the rules: no exchange of money for sexual services, respect quiet hours, clean up after yourself, always obtain consent, no cameras, no drugs or alcohol, and no firearms." Raptor shrugged. "Otherwise, pretty much anything goes."

Jesse refrained from asking about the non-consensuality of exposing everyone in the tub to someone's sperm and lifted himself onto the lip.

Noreen took a deep breath and ducked under the water. Jesse could see her head planted in Sir James crotch. Minutes later, she emerged, swallowed, and took another deep breath. No one showed any reaction, so Jesse decided not to say anything. He supposed if all Sir James' spunk went into Noreen's mouth, none could've gotten into the water.

Baby Girl trudged through the water to Raptor. Standing between her knees, she raised her big brown eyes and gave Raptor a pleading look. Raptor smiled and spread her legs apart. Baby Girl kissed the inside of

Raptor's thighs. Jesse watched fascinated. Although he'd seen Ashleigh and Rachel make out hundreds of time, unless Ashleigh was beating Rachel, they mostly kept covered around him. Baby Girl opened her lips and ran her tongue up and down one of Raptor's thighs from the knee not quite to her crotch then pulled back and repeated her action on the other one. This time, though, when she reached the end of Raptor's leg, baby doll nuzzled her nose into the curly hair. To his embarrassment, Jesse realized he was getting hard. He slipped back into the tub in hopes no one'd notice.

He watched Baby Girl run her tongue through Raptor's slit, eliciting a low moan. Jesse wished he could stroke his cock. One of the rules he remembered that Raptor hadn't mentioned prohibited masturbating to someone else's scene. Even without that, though, he'd be too embarrassed. From the expression on Raptor's face, Baby Girl apparently had found her clit. Jesse had a hard time seeing what she was doing. Raptor had closed her legs around Baby Girl's head. She leaned back and her breathing had gotten fast and irregular. Jesse pressed his lips together to avoid moaning himself. Baby Girl buried her face in Raptor's crotch until she shuddered with orgasm. Then Baby Girl stood higher so she could rest her head on Raptor's lap, wrapping her arms around Raptor's waist.

Jesse heard the clang of someone beating on the metal triangle that hung in the kitchen. Shit, how had eleven o'clock come so soon? "You'll have to excuse me," he said to Dick, not wanting to intrude on the two couples. "I've got to eat before the twelve-thirty classes."

Dick nodded. "See you around, Jess."

Jesse tensed. "It's Jesse, please."

To his surprise, Dick didn't taunt him. "Sorry, Dude. Jesse."

Jesse smiled, reached out a hand and got a firm shake. He went to retrieve his clothing, but decided it better to rinse off so he wouldn't present himself to Lady Tina smelling of chlorine from the hot tub. By the time he struggled into his jeans, and stuck his feet in his shoes, a long line had formed for lunch. Jesse realized he didn't have his plate, but he noticed several people getting one from the kitchen staff so he hoped he could as well rather than have to go all the way back to the tent and start again at the end of the line.

Chapter Twenty-Five

After scarfing down his lunch and running back to the tent for his toothbrush, Jesse arrived at the yurt at precisely twelve-fifteen with his breath minty fresh and his hands shaking.

Lady Tina stood inside, emptying the contents of a small black valise onto a long, white plastic folding table. "Good boy. Set that up for me." She pointed to a massage table folded in half that sat on its side next to the curved canvas wall of the yurt.

Jesse stepped inside the dome. A musty odor emanated from the outdoor carpeting on the platform. He unfolded the table, braced the legs open, and set it upright.

"Sheets in the basket over there." Lady Tina pointed to a green laundry basket to one side of the yurt's double doors.

In addition to clean sheets, the basket contained spray bottles of alcohol and cleaning fluid, paper towels, a box of gloves, a bottle of lube, and a strip of condom packages. Jesse took one sheet and covered the table.

Folks trickled into the yurt and took seats on the chairs arranged in a three-quarter circle around the two tables. Jesse blushed when he realized they would watch him undress. Lady Tina surveyed the collection she had arranged on the one table, then looked at Jesse. "You're still clothed?"

"Sorry, Ma'am, I was waiting for your instructions." Jesse stripped out of his clothing and stood holding it in his hands.

"Set those, there." Lady Tina pointed to a chair at the end of the circle. When he did, she patted the massage table. Jesse sat down and swung his legs up, laying down on his back.

"What's your safeword?" Lady Tina pulled on a pair of nitrile gloves.

"Safeword?"

"Yes, boy. What do you use for a safeword? Or do you just use red?"

"Red, Ma'am."

Lady Tina shook her head, and for a moment it looked as if she'd say something, but then she pressed her lips together. She ran one gloved hand over his chest and he trembled. She lowered her lips to his ear. "Nervous?"

He nodded. "Yes, Ma'am. I've never done this before."

"CBT?" She whispered and her breath tickled his skin.

"Well, I've never had a woman do CBT. And I've never been a stunt bottom."

She smiled, and he wished he could sit with his head in her lap. "You're bisexual?"

"No, Ma'am."

She raised one eyebrow higher than the other which made her look even more beautiful, if that was possible. "I'm gay, Ma'am."

She threw her head back and laughed.

Her reaction confused him. Jesse turned his head to the right and tried to keep his voice low so the others filling the yurt wouldn't hear him. "I've played with lesbians before, Ma'am."

The laughter left her face. She looked at him with brown eyes that had flecks of green in them. "I'm not a lesbian, boy. I'm straight."

Jesse stared at her. "But you just made a play date with Lisbeth?"

"I play with girls, but I don't have sex with them." She looked at her watch. "We'll talk later."

During the class, Jesse couldn't concentrate on Lady Tina's words. She introduced herself and him to the class, and she must have discussed what she intended to cover. The way she had said "We'll talk later" left him too disconcerted to pay attention.

When she pulled the skin of his scrotum to attach clothespins, his breath came in quick shallow gasps. Before she had more than four pinned to his sack, he had a raging hardon which confused him even more. Tony had covered his balls in clothespins on numerous occasions, as many as thirty at one time. Jesse had never once gotten hard.

Lady Tina continued to talk to the class. Her voice caressed Jesse like a familiar song on the radio, but he couldn't distinguish individual words. Every time her gloved fingers touched his skin, the ache in his cock grew more and more intense. She whipped him with a miniflogger and used a Wartenberg wheel on his sensitive skin. Periodically, she'd tweak the clothespins until he almost couldn't stand the pain. Then she removed them, one at a time, smiling when he groaned in agony.

She squeezed his testicles with one hand, grabbed his cock and twisted it with the other. His skinned burned and endorphins raged through him. He couldn't remember anything that had ever turned him on more and he longed for release.

"Boy." Her voice in his ear seemed deafening, although she still whispered. "You know better than to come without permission, don't you?"

"Yes, Ma'am." He wanted to beg for permission, but doubted she'd give it to him in class. He couldn't understand his reaction.

When Lady Tina answered the last question and the workshop finally ended, the class applauded and trickled out. A few stopped by the table and watched while she helped him sit up. She stood between his legs, wrapping her arms around his waist. He leaned his head on her shoulder and inhaled the fragrance of her arousal. He'd spent enough time around Rachel and Ashleigh to recognize the scent, but the aroma that reached his nostrils intoxicated him like nothing he'd ever encountered before. He had an overwhelming urge to know what she tasted like, even though he couldn't imagine why.

Jesse's erection still pained him and he so wished for some kind of relief. But Tony planned to hurt him and he doubted he'd get anytime to himself before he crawled into his sleeping bag. He suppressed a sob.

Lady Tina stepped back and placed her palm against

his cheek. He couldn't remember when she'd removed her gloves. "What makes you think you're gay, boy?"

Startled, he looked up and stared at her.

"Do you like sex with men, boy?" Lady Tina pointed to the basket. "Get me some supplies and help me clean my toys."

Jesse pushed himself off the table and fetched paper towels and the spray bottles.

She sprayed the clothespins and Wartenberg wheel with cleaner. "You don't, do you?"

Jesse used paper towels to wipe each item off before handing it back to her."Ma'am?"

Lady Tina, reached up behind him grabbed his hair and pulled him to his knees. She kept his neck bent back, forcing him to look into her eyes. "Do you like sex with men, boy?"

He squeezed his eyes tight, but the tears seeped out anyway. How had she discovered his secret so easily?

She enfolded him in her arms and pulled him close, his cheek resting against her breasts. He so wanted to lick them, but instead he wrapped his arms tightly around her waist. His breath came in short gasps and he felt on the verge of hiccuping. With one hand, Lady Tina stroked his hair and Jesse longed to transform into a dog so he could sleep at her feet for the rest of his life.

"We need to have a very long conversation, but I have a play date." Lady Tina tipped his chin back with one hand. "You going to the comedy show tonight?"

Tony had said he wanted to, but hadn't mentioned Jesse going with. He probably planned to leave Jesse, deep in subspace, back in the tent. Could Jesse pull out of an endorphin coma for Lady Tina?

"I've a play date, also. I can try to meet you at dinner, but I'm liable to be a little spacey."

"Let's meet after dinner in the library. With most everyone attending the show, we should have the place to ourselves for a long, heart to heart." Lady Tina released him and the loss of her touch left Jesse feeling as if someone had knocked the breath out of him. She turned to pack up her toys, so he stood and folded up the massage table.

When she finally finished, Lady Tina held out her hand. "I appreciate your serving as my stunt bottom. You did very well."

This time Jesse let his lips brush against the soft skin of her fingers. He didn't want to take them away.

"I'll see you at seven-thirty."

"Yes, Ma'am."

Chapter Twenty-Six

As he searched for Tony, Jesse tried to come to terms with his reaction to Lady Tina and to her questioning of his sexuality. He decided she just didn't understand who he was, because she'd only seen him in jeans. For dinner, he'd change into his sundress and the strappy sandals he'd brought to wear with it. Maybe she wanted a doll to play with just like Ashleigh and Rachel. He could be that doll. He wanted to be that doll.

Tony had a boy Jesse had never seen before chained to the standing stone. From the looks of the boy's back, Tony would finish playing with him soon, so Jesse knelt in the grass, out of range of the whip but where Tony could see him. When he noticed Jesse, Tony smiled. A few minutes later, he took the boy down from the stone. Demon showed up with a bottle of water while the boy sucked Tony off. Tony gave the boy to Demon who cuddled him on the other side of the stone. Jesse stripped and stood so Tony could lock him to the chains still encircling the stone.

Because he still had welts from the night before, Tony bound Jesse with his back to the stone. He pulled his four-foot signal whip from the toy bag and kissed Jesse's skin with it. Rather than sinking into subspace this time, Jesse found himself admiring Tony's skill. Several people had gathered around, out of range, to watch. The man had talent. He could throw the whip accurately enough to hit Jesse's nipple, tip of his cock, or where ever else he chose. The pain grew more intense as Tony threw harder and harder. Without the release of subspace, Jesse wanted to squirm in his bindings. Only fear kept him still, fear that any movement would result in the whip landing somewhere it'd cause even more pain.

He could feel endorphins raging through his body, but they had almost no effect, except to sharpen his senses. Memories swirled through his mind of Lady Tina's gloved hand touching his rod and her intoxicating scent. In his head, he heard her voice asking "What makes you think you're gay, boy?" over and over again.

The whip stung his inner thigh and Jesse cried out in pain.

"What's wrong, boy?" Tony stepped up and ran his fingers through Jesse's hair.

Jesse tilted his head, leaning into the caress. "I'm sorry, Sir. I just can't seem to get into subspace."

Tony sighed. "Not like you to get distracted. Not lately, anyway." He pointed to the group of people across the grass unrolling a four-foot wide ribbon of black polyethylene film from the top of the circle to where is sloped down a few yards from the road. "Since you're not exactly enjoying this, guess we'll go join the fun." He unbuckled Jesse and stashed the cuffs and his whips back in the toy bin, leaving the chains on the rock. When Jesse stuck one leg into his jeans, Tony said, "Don't bother putting your clothes on, boy."

"Yes, Sir." Jesse held the jeans and tee shirt so they covered his crotch and followed Tony to the other side of the circle.

The folks who'd stretched out the polyethylene, poured oil from huge bottles onto the plastic. Several naked people lined up at the high end of the strip. Tony headed toward the back of the line and Jesse followed.

Once the oil covered the plastic, the person at the front of the line, a chubby fellow who stood more than six feet tall, jumped forward, landing on his stomach. He slid the length of the plastic, whooping with glee until he skidded into the grass at the end of plastic. "Shit, that part hurt!" The fellow signaled to three of the men standing on either side of the giant slide and they took positions at the end of the plastic. Then he waved to the girl standing next in line. She did an elegant dive onto the plastic, screaming in delight all the way down. Two of the fellows caught her at the end and helped her stand upright.

Jesse chuckled. It looked like fun. When Tony took his turn, he managed to turn around in the middle so that he arrived at far end feet first, receiving cheers from the folks who gathered on either side of the slide. Jesse hesitated before setting his clothes on top of the toy bin where Tony had left his kilt and shirt. At least fifty people had gathered around the slide and lined up behind it. The fear of exposing himself to all of them fought against his desire to try the slide.

Tony stood naked near the bottom of the slide, his

hands crossed over his chest. "C'mon boy, you're holding up the line."

Jesse took a deep breath, set his clothes down, and knelt at the end of the slide. He reached out his arms to lie flat, but didn't move.

An impossibly skinny older woman crouched next to Jesse's face. "You need a running start to get some momentum. You want a push?"

Jesse blushed and pulled himself forward with his arms. By the time he reached the bottom, he was panting from the exertion and covered in oil.

Tony offered him a hand to help him stand. "Go give it another try, boy. This time for real."

"Yes, Sir." Jesse watched the older woman run toward the plastic, and land on her ass. She slid all the way down sitting upright. He decided to try her approach -- it looked more comfortable than landing on his privates.

The line now stretched almost to the vendor's area near their camp. Jesse watched the various approaches and admired the bodies getting covered with slick oil. Young, old, skinny, fat, no one seemed worried about what others thought of how they looked. By the time he reached the front of the line again, Jesse no longer held his hands over his crotch, but let them hang by his side.

He took several steps back and ran toward the slick plastic, doing a cannonball and landing on his ass. It hurt, especially because of the welts Tony had left the night before. But Jesse giggled as he slid down the slope into the arms of the two fellows at the end. The ride left him giddy and it took a moment before he could walk over to Tony without tripping over his own feet. "May I go take a shower, Sir?"

Tony nodded. "Get my towel and kit, too. We both need to wash up before dinner."

"Yes, Sir." Jesse carried the toys and clothes back to the tent and emerged with his and Tony's shower gear. He followed Tony through the camp until he stopped in front of a row of shower heads and faucets sticking out of a wooden wall.

Jesse sighed. He supposed expecting a private place to bathe was asking too much. He hung up their towels and handed Tony his kit.

Tony didn't reach for it. "Bathe me."

Jesse blinked. Tony had never told him to do anything like that before. "Yes, Sir." He unzipped the cammy green bag and removed Tony's shampoo and Irish Spring soap. Tony stepped in front of one of the showers and Jesse turned the water on.

He poured some of the Crew shampoo into his palm, releasing the scent of sage and rosemary and massaged it into Tony's scalp. Jesse found himself wondering what kind of shampoo Lady Tina used, but shook his head to chase away the thought. Tony didn't tolerate inattention. After he rinsed the shampoo from Tony's hair, Jesse scrubbed him with the bar of soap. When Jesse soaped up Tony's genitals, his cock got hard. Jesse put the soap away, rinsed Tony, and turned off the water.

Kneeling in water swirling toward the drain, Jesse took Tony in his mouth, doing his best not to gag on the taste of soap. Tony lasted longer than usual and Jesse's knees hurt from the cement under them. His throat ached and he wondered if licking pussy was as uncomfortable as sucking cock. Squeezing Tony's shaft with one hand, he caressed his scrotum with the other, and sucked as hard as he could on the glans, trying to make Tony come. Finally, Jesse could feel Tony's balls tighten, but the man pulled out of his mouth. For a moment, Jesse despaired that Tony would try to delay his orgasm to keep Jesse on his knees even longer. Much to his relief, Tony spurted all over his face, sparing him from having to swallow. He wondered how much fluid a woman produced and whether swallowing that would be as distasteful.

Jesse cleaned off the tip of Tony's cock with his tongue and stood up to get him his towel.

Tony, dried off and wrapped the towel around his waist. "You can take your shower now, boy. I'll see you at dinner."

"May I please wear the dress you let me bring for dinner, Sir?"

Tony scowled. "I suppose. But you only get to wear it this one evening."

"Yes, Sir. Thank you, Sir." Jesse opened his own kit as Tony strode off. After scrubbing the oil off his skin with vanilla moisturizing body wash and shampooing his hair with raspberry & jojoba, Jesse toweled dry and hurried back to the tent. He heard the first dinner bell clang, but didn't rush because he had at least an hour before his own shift started.

Once he'd put on the pink and purple sundress, a pair of matching purple panties, and the pink sandals, Jesse felt presentable for the first time since he'd arrived at the campgrounds. Sitting cross-legged on the floor of the tent, he propped his mirror on his knees so he could apply eye liner and mascara. More than that, he feared, would upset Tony. He draped the fringed gold shawl over his shoulders and headed for the kitchen. He was halfway there when he turned around and went back. Jesse rummaged in his suitcase until he found the one pair of earrings he'd brought. Threading the wires through his earlobes, Jesse smiled. The earrings, a chain of metallic pink hearts, brushed his shoulders. He hoped Lady Tina would appreciate his outfit, but if she didn't, at least she'd understand who he was.

Chapter Twenty-Seven

One hand clutching the shawl and the other balancing his and Tony's plates, Jesse stepped carefully to avoid catching the heels of his sandals in the grass. Someone had removed the polyethylene, and the only reminder of the afternoon's hilarity was the puddle of oil where the slide had ended. Jesse gave it a wide berth to avoid soiling his shiny shoes.

He found Tony standing in line with Demon and handed over his plate and cup.

Demon winked at Jesse. "You look lovely tonight. Hot date?"

Jesse felt his cheeks get red.

Tony raised one eyebrow and gave Jesse a slow once over. "Who *did* you dress up for?"

Fortunately, Tony reached the front of the line at that moment and turned his attention to the servers behind the counter. Rather than cut in, Jesse slunk to the end of the line, grateful to put as much distance as he could between himself and Tony for the moment.

Dinner required assembly, made difficult by the shawl around his shoulders. From the counter, he received two taco shells filled with ground turkey and black beans, along with a large serving of Spanish rice. But he had to add the tomatoes, lettuce, grated cheese, olives, sour cream, and salsa. After trying to juggle plate, serving spoons, and still keep his shawl draped around his shoulders, Jesse gave up and set the plate down on one corner of the table while he heaped everything onto it. Fortunately, he remembered to stop himself before adding onions.

Jesse grabbed several napkins and stopped at the hospitality tent for a cup of coffee before seeking a seat in the crowded dining area. He found an empty place at a table occupied by three rather large young women and a barrel chested older fellow with bushy silver hair and a full beard. The women all wore steel rings around their neck.

"Hi there." One of the women said as he sat down. "You new here?"

Jesse nodded and set his plate on the table in front of him, spreading one of the napkins across his lap.

"This is my master, Bradley, my sister slaves Lilith and Callie." She pointed to the two women sitting across from Jesse. "I'm Serenity."

Jesse nodded his head at each. "I'm Jesse from Eugene. I got in last night. It's my first time."

"We've come every year since '01." She smiled. You enjoying yourself?"

Jesse tilted his head to one side. He had to think

about his answer. "Some of it's been fun. Some a little overwhelming."

"If it helps," Lilith said laughing, "you're not alone feeling like that."

"It does get better," Callie said standing. "I'm going to get my Master and my sisters some spice cake for dessert. Would you like me to get a piece for you also?"

Jesse grinned. He hadn't seen the cake. "That'd be great, thanks." He sipped at his coffee. It tasted vile, probably leftover from breakfast, but he wanted to be alert for his meeting with Lady Tina.

Piling their plates up at the end of the table, Serenity asked, "What part have you liked best."

Jesse thought it better not to mention his experience with Lady Tina. "The slide was lots of fun."

"First year we've had that," Lilith said. "Someone donated all the Visqueen and oil."

"You went down twice, didn't you?" Serenity took her Master's coffee cup. "Be right back." She headed for the hospitality tent.

"Coffee always this bad?" Jesse grimaced as he finished the contents of his cup and then scraped his plate with his fork to get enough meat and sour cream to cover the taste.

" 'pends on who's making it," Bradley said. "Usually it's tolerable, but that's part of why the espresso bar sets up shop next to the house. Those who care about coffee either bring their own or buy it from Adrienne."

"Adrienne?" Jesse wiped his fingers and mouth with a napkin.

Bradley accepted the cup from Serenity. "Miss the talent show last night?"

Callie returned balancing five plates of cake and set one in front of each of them.

Jesse nodded and licked the salsa off his fork before dipping it into the moist cake.

Bradley sipped at his coffee. "Andy, who owns Coffee Temple, moonlights as drag queen Adrienne." Jesse noted he didn't seem to mind the taste. Of course, from the light brown color, Serenity had added plenty of creamer and probably sugar as well. "Puts on quite a show."

Jesse nodded, but the delicate flavors of cinnamon, nutmeg and cloves in the cake captured his attention. "Wow, this is good."

"Food was always great, but the last two years, we've had a pro for lead cook." Taking a fork full of cake, Lilith smiled. "We've all gotten quite spoiled."

Jesse savored another bite.

"Hey, everyone." A short, balding man stood with a microphone on the stage at the far end of the dining area. "Having a great time?"

Hoots, cheers, applause, and shouts answered him.

"Got a few announcements for you." He perched a pair of readers on his nose. "Tonight, for your entertainment pleasure, we'll welcome Seattle favorite Candy Cane and her comedic crew right here on this very stage. Prepare to laugh your socks off. Oh, shoot, most of you aren't wearing any."

The diners around Jesse chuckled.

The man on the stage flipped the papers in his hand. "The kitchen crew would like to remind you that the big blue cans are for recycling, not garbage. Trash goes in the green cans. Don't forget, quiet time starts at ten o'clock.

Tomorrow's workshop on caning's been cancelled due to an illness. Instead, we'll have a workshop on Florentine flogging -- same time and place. Always remember to check the bulletin board across from the kitchen for last minute schedule changes. Any other announcements?"

Jesse saw Serenity raise her hand and stand. "We're having a fund-raising raffle tomorrow night. Prizes are on display in the volunteer coordinator's tent across from the hospitality tent. Tickets are a dollar each or six for five dollars. The proceeds go to the foundation." She sat back down.

No one else offered any announcements.

"Okay, folks, see you back here at eight o'clock for Candy Cane and her comedic crew." The man turned off the mike and put it back in a stand in the middle of the stage.

Jesse looked at his watch. "Excuse me, I've got to go meet someone. Thanks for the cake." He took his dishes and headed for the wash station. Fortunately, he didn't see any sign of Tony, so he only had to worry about his own. He returned them to the tent and headed for the house. Half round logs covered the exterior of the building, as long as the high school gymnasium back in Eugene. French doors, the glass opaqued by steam, led into an enclosed swimming pool area. Jesse realized he had no idea where to find the library.

He turned back toward the espresso tent and saw Lady Tina perched on one of two sofas that faced each other under the canopy. Across from her sat the baldheaded guy who'd eaten dinner in the stone circle, puffing on a cigarette. An espresso machine steamed and spit, drowning out the music that played from a small boom box hanging from one of the tent poles.

Lady Tina looked at the silver watch on her wrist. "Gotta go, Snakeman, I promised this boy a conversation. Thanks for the coffee." She smiled at the bald guy, who took her hand and kissed her fingers.

Jesse stepped aside and followed Lady Tina past the swimming pool entrances to a door in the middle of the building. When he saw that's where she was headed, he scurried in front of her so he could open the door. They entered a room bigger than his entire apartment. Floor to ceiling shelves filled with books lined the far wall, a sectional sofa curved around in front of a stone fireplace, and several other cushy chairs were scattered about. In one corner at the back of the room, stood two tall stacks of metal chairs. Three closed doors offered access to the rest of the house.

Lady Tina settled into a green arm chair near the fireplace, put her paper coffee cup on the low, carved wooden table against the wall, and pointed to the footstool in front of it. Jesse sat on the edge, his hands in his lap.

"You look quite lovely tonight, boy." She crossed one long leg over the other. Jesse noticed her toenails were painted dark red. "Did you dress up for me?"

"Well, yes, Ma'am. I thought it might help you understand my," he paused and cleared his throat, "situation a little better."

Lady Tina threw her head back against the chair and laughed. For some reason, Jesse found himself quite taken with how pretty it sounded. "Oh, I think I understand you better than you do yourself. You like wearing girls clothing, yes?"

Jesse nodded.

"You played with dolls when you were a child? You're effeminate?"

Jesse gulped and nodded again. Somehow when she said that word, it carried none of the torment and chastisement others spewed out with it.

"Have you ever wished you were a woman, that you didn't have a penis?"

Jesse pursed his lips together. He tucked or wore a gaff when his outfit required it. The sundress had a full skirt so he hadn't bothered. He savored any opportunity to masturbate and if he concentrated he could enjoy a blow job on those rare occasions when Tony let Demon or Shane suck him. He shook his head. No, he liked his penis just fine.

"Have you ever enjoyed sex with a man?" Lady Tina stared at him and he felt himself wanting to be one of the green flecks floating in the brown pools of her irises.

Jesse lowered his eyes. Lady Tina grabbed his hair, pulled him off the footstool onto his knees. "I asked you a question, boy." Despite the way she held his head bent back, her words held no menace. Her soft voice offered comfort and understanding. Jesse's lower lip trembled.

Chapter Twenty-Eight

"Why do you think you're gay, boy?" Lady Tina kept his head back with one hand tangled in his hair, but her other hand cupped his cheek and he leaned into her touch.

Knowing he'd burst into tears if he tried to speak, he shrugged his shoulders.

"You're going to have to do better than that. It's okay if you cry." Without releasing his hair, she produced a box of tissues from somewhere and set it on the table where he could reach it.

"I've always been gay." Jesse choked on his words. He reached for a tissue and dabbed at his eyes. It came away with black smears.

"Says who?"

"Everyone."

"Your parents?"

Jesse nodded.

Lady Tina released his hair so quickly he almost fell

backwards. She kicked the footstool hard enough for it to skid across the room where it slammed into the wall.

A few seconds later, the door burst open and Snakeman stood there naked, his erection jutting out. "What the fuck?"

"Sorry to interrupt you, Snakeman." Lady Tina sat back down in the armchair. "Just getting rid of some anger. Go back to," she glanced at his cock, "your lady."

Snakeman looked at the footstool, locked eyes with Lady Tina for what seemed like minutes, then slammed the door closed.

Lady Tina patted her leg and let Jesse rest his head there. He couldn't think of anything more sublime. She even stroked his hair.

"I'm just so very tired of people assuming any effeminate male is gay."

Jesse inhaled, but the heavenly aroma of the afternoon didn't permeate his nostrils. Instead, he only smelled the leather of her skirt.

"You ever had sex with a woman, boy?"

Jesse wanted to shake his head, but he didn't want to lift it off the exquisitely soft skin of Lady Tina's leg to do so. "No, Ma'am."

"Have you ever wanted to?"

Jesse thought about all the times he'd watched Ashleigh and Rachel together and wished they'd include him. "Only with lesbians, Ma'am."

Lady Tina chuckled. "You want to explain that, boy?"

"My two best friends, the ones who introduced me to S&M, were a lesbian couple. I used to get turned on watching them together."

"Were?" Lady Tina ran her fingers through his hair

over and over again and Jesse hoped she'd never stop. "They aren't your best friends now?"

"Ashleigh got a job in Seattle and I never get to see them anymore."

"Ashleigh Lester?"

"Yes, Ma'am."

"I know her. She's manages the Hot Topics store in Auburn. Small world. She'll be here tomorrow and Monday, by the way. Don't know if you knew that. I think her current girlfriend's name is Linda, though."

Jesse sat up, then immediately returned his head to Lady Tina's lap. "No, Ma'am. I didn't even know I'd be here until I arrived."

Lady Tina made a sound in her throat that Jesse couldn't have described if he wanted to. "Tell me about this person who decides where you go and who you play with, but who apparently isn't your master."

Jesse shrugged. "Tony doesn't let anyone call him master. He prefers Sir."

"But he tells you what to wear and who to play with?"

Jesse wondered how she knew that Tony didn't like him wearing dresses.

"You'd have worn girl's clothing since you arrived if Tony hadn't told you not to, yes?"

Jesse blinked. Could Lady Tina read his mind? "Yes, Ma'am."

Lady Tina tightened her grip on his hair and lifted his head until he was forced to look her in the eyes. "You're not gay, boy. You're a straight sissy."

He started to protest, but she put one finger on her lips. "Just 'cause you like to wear dresses doesn't make you gay. Wanting to have sex with men, enjoying sex with men makes you gay." A tear appeared at the corner of her eyes and Jesse worried that he'd upset her. "You poor boy. How old are you?"

"Nineteen, Ma'am."

"You've been sexually active how long?"

"Since I turned eighteen, Ma'am."

"I can't believe you've spent your entire life ..." She sighed. "I bet you hate sex and do just about anything to avoid it?"

Jesse lowered his eyes, although he couldn't drop his chin because Lady Tina still gripped his hair. His bottom lip trembled again.

Soft lips touched his and he could taste the coffee Lady Tina drank earlier. He opened his eyes wide in surprise and his breath became raspy.

"Do you practice safe sex, boy?"

Jesse gurgled, he couldn't find the words to answer her question.

"Do you only have sex with the one man?"

Jesse shook his head. "Sometimes I have oral sex with one of his other boys."

"Do they use condoms?"

Jesse swallowed. "He almost never..." he paused not knowing what word would be appropriate to use. "Mostly, I just give blow jobs. Sometimes he has one of the others give me one."

The smile on Lady Tina's face reminded him, for a moment, of his mother's tight-lipped disapproval. "Does he use a condom when he takes you in the ass?"

Jesse nodded. That'd been a long hard battle. But when Jesse explained he had promised his dad, Tony had accepted Jesse's one requirement..

"Who else does he have sex with?"

"Demon and Shane."

"Does he use condoms with them?"

Jesse shook his head. "But none of us have sex with anyone else." Jesse thought of the boy Tony played with earlier in the afternoon. "Not usually, anyway. And Tony insists his boys get tested twice a year."

"When's the last time you were tested?"

"Two months ago, Ma'am. All negative." Jesse didn't understand why she asked him all these questions. He just wanted her to let go of his hair so he could rest his cheeks against her legs again.

Lady Tina sat for a minute with a pensive look on her face. Then she kissed him again, drawing her tongue across his lips. To his embarrassment, Jesse felt himself harden under his skirt. When he looked down, he could see himself tenting the fabric. Lady Tina lowered her eyes to look at his crotch and laughed. "That's what I thought."

She released Jesse and stood up. "Put the footstool back, boy."

"Yes, Ma'am." Confused, Jesse picked up the stool and set it in front of the chair.

Lady Tina grabbed a handful of condoms from one of the ever-present plastic bowls. She pointed to her coffee cup. "Get rid of that." Jesse looked around and found a trash can nearby.

"Come along, boy. We're going to find out just how gay you are." Lady Tina stood in front of the door until Jesse opened it for her.

They stepped out into the now dark night. The air had a touch of chill and Jesse pulled his shawl tighter around his shoulders. He realized Lady Tina only wore a short sleeved blouse over her leather skirt. "Excuse me, Ma'am. Are you cold? Would you like my shawl."

Lady Tina turned to him and he could see her smile in the porch light. "Thank you, boy. You are a sweetie."

Jesse draped the shawl over her shoulders and she rewarded him with a kiss on his cheek. He wondered what doing things for her would be like. Ashleigh and Rachel often let him clean their house and make them treats. Sometimes he even got to give them massages. Until he let Jesse bathe him earlier, Tony only wanted Jesse to take his beatings or blow him. Jesse missed the smile he would get when he pleased the girls.

Chapter Twenty-Nine

Jesse followed Lady Tina across the stone circle to a path that led away from the kitchen. He could hear laughter and applause coming from the stage area. When they left the circle of light near the road, Lady Tina paused for a moment. "Put your hand on my shoulder, boy, and try not to stumble." She stood still for a moment after he did as instructed. Under his shawl, he could feel the rounded shape of her shoulder. He had an inexplicable urge to kiss it.

She led the way through the dark. Jesse could make out glimpses of tents on either side. Lanterns hanging from canopy poles and tree branches provided enough light for him to pick his way through the dew dampened grass. Lady Tina stopped in front of a large domed tent and leaned down to unzip the front. She stepped inside and Jesse waited for her to return his shawl. He heard the hiss of propane and the click of a lighter. A light flickered on inside the tent.

"Come on in, boy."

He ducked his head to step through the opening.

"Zip it up so the mosquitoes don't follow you."

He complied then turned to find Lady Tina laying on her side on a blow up mattress covered with a double sleeping bag. She was propped up on one elbow, and he thought she looked like a goddess lounging in her temple. The only thing missing was a bunch of grapes for him to peel and offer her.

Jesse felt out of place standing inside the tent. "Would you like me to get you something, Ma'am?"

"The only thing I have an appetite for right now, is you, boy." Lady Tina patted mattress in front of her.

Jesse knelt on the ground."Ma'am?"

"Boy, are you a complete innocent?"

Jesse opened his eyes wider.

"Never mind. That pretty much answers my question." Lady Tina reached out her hand and slid it behind Jesse's neck, pulling his face toward hers. She kissed him, thrusting her tongue deep into his mouth. At first, Jesse didn't know what to do. He couldn't believe this beautiful woman wanted him and the idea that he desired her appalled him. But he couldn't deny his reaction. He was panting heavily and his erection already poked through the leg of his panties.

With one hand still on the back of his neck, Lady Tina guided Jesse's face to her neck. Her skin tasted of almond oil. Jesse sighed with pleasure and kissed his way from her ear to her throat. He could feel her pulse against his lips and, for a moment, he got lost in its rhythm. Lady Tina slid her fingers into his hair, lifted his head, and pointed his face toward her feet.

Jesse unclasped the black leather straps from around her ankles and slid the sandals off. He set them on the floor of the tent at the foot of her bed and admired her shapely painted toes and graceful arch. She lifted one foot slightly above the other and Jesse lowered his mouth to that one. Her feet tasted a bit earthier than the rest of her, but he still enjoyed the soft skin against his lips. He kissed the tops, then licked her toes.

Lady Tina shifted slightly and sighed with what he hoped was pleasure. Holding her heels in his hands, he licked each of her toes in succession. The sound that emerged from her throat, a deep moan, left no doubt that she enjoyed the attention, so he sucked on the big toe of her right foot. As he did, Jesse noticed the return of the intoxicating aroma he'd enjoyed that afternoon. The thought that Lady Tina got aroused by him sucking on her toes made Jesse so hard he ached.

More than anything now, he wanted to taste what he could smell. He licked his way from her toes to the inside of her ankle, wondering just how much she'd permit. Then he remembered all the questions she'd asked him about sex and condoms. She *wanted* him to service her sexually. Jesse couldn't decide how he should take that. Lady Tina had never asked him if he wanted to have sex with her. She apparently just assumed that he did.

She was right.

Right now he would do anything to taste her, to please her. He wanted to make her come the way Rachel had done Ashleigh, the way Baby Girl had done Raptor. And he'd absolutely no idea how to proceed.

Lady Tina sighed as Jesse kissed the inside of one thigh from knee to just below her silky black panties.

He did the same on the other, sliding his parted lips and his extended tongue along her sweetly smooth skin.

"You may take them off, boy." Lady Tina put her feet flat on the bed and raised her hips enough so he could ease her panties down her legs.

Jesse stared at the curly auburn hair that glistened with moisture. Lady Tina put one ankle behind his neck and pulled his face down. He took a deep breath, inhaling her tantalizing essence and nuzzled his nose into the hair until he found her lips. He stuck out his tongue and lapped at the nectar flowing from between them and almost fainted at the exquisite taste. Jesse felt himself slipping into subspace, a place he'd never ventured without the help of pain. He whimpered, wanting to indulge, wanting to please, not knowing what to do next.

"Just lick your way in, boy. I want your tongue everywhere, but give your primary attention to my clit, this little spot right here."

Jesse put his hands on either side of her bush and gently pried her outer lips apart to find the place her manicured fingertip indicated. Inside he found the most beautiful rose he'd ever seen, shimmering in the lantern light. The delicate pink folds led inward to her opening and at the top, he could see what must be her clit poking out from the surrounding flesh. He slid his tongue along the slit, tasting her juices, reveling in the exquisite satin. With a moan, he licked again and again, sucking in her honey, pushing into her hole, nuzzling the little button at the top of it all.

Floating in the surreality of subspace, his mouth and nose full of ambrosia, Jesse knew he'd found heaven.

With her hand on the back of his head, Lady Tina pushed him tighter against her. He sucked on her clit until she trembled and even more nectar flowed from her. Inebriated, he licked and sucked and licked some more only to have her tremble again and give him more and more elixir.

Moaning with the exquisite joy of what she offered, Jesse resisted when Lady Tina tugged at his hair. He'd never get enough of the delights between her legs and he tried to burrow his face deeper.

Lady Tina chuckled and Jesse wondered what amused her. On the one hand, he wanted to please her and he enjoyed the sound of her laughter. On the other, he didn't want anything distract him from his feast. She gasped and came again, then yanked on his hair until the pain made him lift his head. Lady Tina pulled him up by his hair until he lay stretched out next to her on the mattress.

Releasing him, she grabbed one of the condoms from where she had left them beside the bed and handed it to him. "Put it on."

Jesse just stared at her, the condom gripped in his fingers. "Ma'am?"

"Oh, good grief." Lady Tina took the packet back, ripped it open, and pushed up his skirt so she could roll the latex over his throbbing erection poking out of the leg of his panties.

He'd forgotten about his hardon in his exquisite indulgence of the offering between her legs, but her touch made him only too aware of how long it'd been since he'd had a chance to jerk off. He groaned.

Lady Tina swung one leg over his pelvis, grabbed

his cock, and slid it inside of her. Jesse's eyes closed and his mouth fell open. He'd never experienced anything so divine in his entire life. She lifted herself up and slid back down. Jesse felt his balls tighten. "Ma'am, I'm so sorry, I don't think I can hold back. This is just too intense."

She smiled at him. "Because it's your first time, just this once I'm going to let you come without restriction. But I expect you to get it up again right away so I can use it for my pleasure."

Jesse wanted to assure her of his desire to please, but he couldn't speak. She rose up and down on his cock once more and he exploded with a cry.

Lady Tina laughed. "Still think you're gay, boy?" she whispered. She sat on his cock, her muscles clenching around him. He never even softened, just stayed hard. Watching his face, she moved up and down again and Jesse got lost in the bliss of her wetness sliding against his shaft.

"You had your one shot, boy." Lady Tina's voice cracked slightly. "Next time you wait for permission."

"Yes, Ma'am." Jesse didn't want to come. He wanted to stay hard forever so Lady Tina could take her pleasure from him.

Her breathing got more and more ragged. Jesse opened his eyes so he could watch her face. With her eyes closed, her lips slightly parted, she looked exquisitely beautiful. Suddenly she jerked forward and fell onto her hands, her breasts hanging down to brush against his chest. Instinctively, Jesse placed on hand on each of her hips and thrust himself up into her until her whole body trembled, her muscles clenching around his cock, and she dropped onto him. He felt enveloped in her weight and warmth and floated in the euphoria of her scent. If he licked his lips, he could taste her too.

Lady Tina stayed on his chest until she stopped panting, then rolled to his side, landing on her back next to him. Jesse longed for more contact, something he'd never wanted after sex before. After a man fucked him, Jesse was just grateful to have it over with. Now he yearned for Lady Tina's touch even though only an inch separated them.

Carefully, he turned on his side, narrowing that distance. He almost sobbed with relief when she slid her arm under his neck and brought his head to rest on her shoulder. Pressing his lips together, hoping he didn't act too boldly, Jesse slid his arm across Lady Tina's waist. Much to his delight, she put her other palm on his forearm. Snuggled next to her, Jesse drifted in ecstatic bliss. Her breathing became heavy and regular and he realized she'd drifted off to sleep. He knew he should return to his tent. Tony would wonder what had become of him. But Jesse couldn't leave without disturbing Lady Tina, and he really had no desire to be anywhere else.

Chapter Thirty

The smell of baking muffins woke Jesse. He blinked his eyes and realized daylight suffused the tent, dimming the glow from the lamp.

Lady Tina smiled at him. "You never answered my question, boy."

"Ma'am?"

"Still think you're gay?"

Jesse felt his cheeks get hot. Much to his chagrin, his cock got hard. "No, Ma'am. Thank you for showing me my error." Jesse thought of all the guys he had dated, all the sex he had endured and frowned.

"You can't change the past, boy." Lady Tina pushed his head toward her waist. "But you can try to make up for lost time."

Jesse smiled and backed up slightly. He kissed the cleft between her breasts and much to his delight, she unbuttoned her blouse. Licking the flesh available above her lacy black bra, Jesse struggled with the clasp between the luscious mounds. She pushed his clumsy fingers aside and undid it herself, pulling the cups away to reveal delectable nipples surrounded by light brown circles, dark against the pale skin of her breasts.

He licked them erect and then sucked gently. She ran her fingers through his tangled hair and sighed. Jesse caressed one breast with his palm while his mouth attended the other. He alternated between them until Lady Tina pushed his head lower. He slid his lips along her belly to the ambrosia between her legs. It tasted a bit muskier than the night before, but he still loved the flavor. How could he have lived without this delight for so very long?

After she came twice, Lady Tina pulled his head up by his hair and looked him in the eye. "Your appetite's quite appreciated, boy, but I have got to pee." She let go of his hair and grabbed panties and a pair of shorts from the duffle bag at the head of the mattress. "I think we should continue this *conversation*," she winked at him, "after breakfast."

"Yes, Ma'am." Jesse felt the blood drain from his cheeks. What if he ran into Tony?

Lady Tina pressed her lips to his forehead. "Don't worry, boy. I'll explain what's going on to whoever you came here with. And, we really do need to have a detailed conversation. I want to know more about how you ended up in this predicament." She took a camisole from the bag and pulled it on over her head, tossing the blouse and her bra on the bed. "Don't need to be obvious that you didn't return to your own tent last night. Leave your dress here for now and wrap your shawl around your waist."

"Yes, Ma'am." Jesse did as instructed, tying a knot in the fabric over his left hip while Lady Tina turned off the lamp.

Lady Tina ran her fingers through her hair and he did the same. He climbed out of the tent behind her, turning back to zip the entrance closed. He followed her to the toilets and waited for her after he relieved himself and washed his hands. They borrowed plates from the kitchen crew and she let him carry hers to one of the picnic tables. After she sat down, she handed him her coffee cup."Creamer, no sugar."

Jesse scurried to the hospitality tent and filled their cups. When he returned, the blonde woman from the day before sat next to Lady Tina. Jesse felt a twinge of jealousy. But, then he remembered that Lady Tina had said she was straight. *And so are you*, said the voice in his head. Jesse ignored it, set the cup down in front of Lady Tina, and stood in front of his own plate. She smiled and nodded at him. Then he took his seat.

He found the muffins particularly yummy this morning. Even the coffee didn't taste half bad. After devouring the muffins and oatmeal with raisins and brown sugar, Jesse found he still had an appetite. "May I go get some more, Ma'am?"

Lady Tina smiled at him. "Yes, boy. And bring me another cup of coffee."

"Yes, Ma'am. Thank you, Ma'am." Jesse practically skipped back to the kitchen.

Tony stood at the counter, putting muffins on his plate. Jesse froze. *Not really hungry.* He turned on his heel toward the refuge of the hospitality tent.

"Boy!" Tony bellowed.

Jesse's lower lip trembled and he tried to hold back the tears. "Yes, Sir?"

Tony walked toward him, plate filled with muffins and oatmeal in one hand, empty cup dangling from his little finger. "Where the hell have you been?"

Jesse swallowed. Before he could answer a sweet voice rang out from his elbow.

"I'm sorry, I don't see a collar on this boy's neck. Do you own him?"

Tony stared at Lady Tina for what seemed like ten minutes. "Owning humans isn't legal. I'm his Sir."

"And, as such, do you believe it appropriate to embarrass him in front of everyone," Lady Tina waved a hand at the folks getting their breakfast and washing up, "by demanding to know his whereabouts."

Tony glowered at her. "Just who do you think you are, Lady? I'm the one wondering what the hell happened to him. Had my other boys crawling around this place with flashlights looking for him half the night."

Lady Tina nodded. "My apologies. I should have had him let you know he was going to spend the night with me." She spoke so quietly, Jesse almost couldn't make out what she was saying. But the expression on Tony's face made it clear he heard every word. "We need to have a conversation." Lady Tina nodded at Jesse. "The three of us."

"Lady, I don't know why you think my relationship with this boy is any of your business or that you have any right to spend time with him without my permission ..."

"Let's take this over there." Lady Tina pointed behind the hospitality tent to an open area surrounded by the backs of the dining canopy, stage, and kitchen storage tent.

Jesse wanted nothing more than to dig a hole he could crawl into, but he followed. Tony stomped ahead of them all. Lady Tina stepped gracefully between all the stakes and rope.

Tony turned on his heel and crossed his arms over his chest, holding his plate over one elbow. "Not that it's any of your concern, but I've watched over this boy for the last few months, ever since those two dykes dumped him on me when they moved up here. He's not exactly my type, but I took him into my family 'cause he's got no one else. Why the hell, you think this is any of your business..."

Jesse just stared at Tony, unable to speak, barely able to think.

Lady Tina tilted her head to one side. "It appears that we both have one thing in common, at least. We both care about what happens to Jesse."

Tony grumbled, but he nodded.

"I suspect his problems started long before you got involved."

"Problems?"

"Jesse's straight."

Tony's plate tipped and its contents slid into the sand. His jaw dropped and his face got red. His eyebrows scrunched together then relaxed. Tony finally turned to Jesse, his knuckles on his hips, the empty plate pointing straight down.

"Boy?"

Jesse burst into tears.

Lady Tina tugged his head against her shoulder, and

he resisted throwing his arms around her waist. "It's not his fault. Everyone assumes if a boy's effeminate and likes to wear girls' clothing he must be gay."

"Are you telling me that you and he ..." Tony looked like he wanted to puke. He didn't wait for an answer. "I want you out of my tent, boy."

"No problem. He can spend the rest of the weekend in mine."

Tony's eyes narrowed. "And how does he expect to get home?"

Lady Tina smiled. "There's lots of folks here from Eugene. I'm sure we can find him a ride."

"Sir, I'm sorry I've disappointed you." Jesse dropped to his knees in front of Tony.

Tony let out a long slow breath. "I wouldn't say that, boy. If you are straight, it's not like you can help it. Although I can't for the life of me understand how you couldn't figure that out for yourself. Regardless, you've served me well under the circumstances." Tony patted his head. "But, you understand I can't have a straight boy in my family?"

"Of course, Sir. Thank you for keeping an eye on me."

"Just don't embarrass me, boy."

"No, Sir, I'd never ..."

Lady Tina stepped up close to him and Jesse wrapped his arms around her legs. She ran her fingers through his hair. "Come, let's go get your things."

When he struggled to his feet, she strode away, heading around the kitchen toward the stone circle.

Jesse hesitated long enough to grab Tony's dropped muffins and scoop up what he could of the oatmeal, then scampered after her, dumping everything in the first trash can he passed and brushing his hands together trying to remove the sand while he followed Lady Tina. She didn't pause until they reached the vendor's area. "Where's your tent, boy?"

"I thought you knew, Ma'am. You seemed sure of where you were going." He led the way through the campground.

"Just figured you were camped with the Eugene crowd. I take it that's the person you've been going to for permission, the one who wouldn't let you wear what you like?"

Jesse pressed his lips together and nodded. He unzipped the tent. "I'll just be a minute." He didn't think Tony would appreciate it he allowed Lady Tina into his tent. Demon and Shane probably wouldn't like it either. Jesse stepped inside, scooped up his suitcase, retrieved his towel from where it hung from one of the tent poles, and made sure he had everything. He left the sleeping bag. It was Tony's anyway. He hoped Lady Tina would let him sleep in her arms again tonight.

When he stepped outside, he found Lady Tina talking to Lady Nell.

"Not a problem, Tina. But I'm here until Tuesday."

"So am I. Decided to help with take down this year since I don't go back to work until Thursday."

"Excellent. Then it's settled. Thanks."

The two Dommes hugged and then Lady Tina headed back toward her tent. "Let's stash your stuff and go get a shower. I think I've got something you can wear for today at least."

"Ma'am, may I ask you a question?" Jesse stopped, but Lady Tina kept walking so he had to scurry to catch up.

She didn't answer until they reached her tent. "After we shower." She pointed to the zipper and Jesse juggled his things so he could open it for her. "There's a class I want to take late this afternoon, but until then I've cancelled my play dates so we can find someplace private to talk."

Jesse stepped aside so Lady Tina could enter the tent. "Yes, Ma'am."

"Stick your stuff over there. Bring just your kit and your towel." Lady Tina extracted her own kit from her duffle, as well as another pair of shorts and another black camisole. Jesse wondered how many she owned. The one she wore now had a different neckline than the one she had on the other day. That had a lace inset, this plunged deeper revealing the luscious cleavage he'd had the privilege of exploring such a very short time ago.

Lady Tina didn't walk in the direction of the showers he and Tony had used. Instead, Jesse followed her around the stone circle to the house. She entered through the French doors to the pool area, through a narrow passageway on the far side that led to a bathroom with a small shower stall. She pointed to the sink. "You can brush your teeth and shave while I shower."

Jesse had time to do both and he still waited quite a while before Lady Tina turned off the water and pulled the shower curtain aside. He handed her the towel she'd brought. She dried her hair and wrapped the towel around herself, then let Jesse trade places with her. Although he tried to be quick, he found Lady Tina had dressed and dried her hair before he emerged from the shower. He wondered if she wore makeup at home, although she certainly didn't need any. Her skin glowed and dark lashes fringed her beautiful eyes.

After he dried off, she handed him a straight black dress with spaghetti straps. "This should fit you."

Jesse wiggled into it. He wished he had his gaff, the dress clung to the bulge in front. "Thank you, Ma'am. Perhaps I could find some tape somewhere so I can tuck things away.

Lady Tina looked him up and down and smiled. "Nope. I like it this way. Going out in public, I'd want a smoother line." She looked up with a wicked glint in her eyes, running her hand down his chest and across his groin.

Jesse felt his cheeks get hot and his cock harden.

She laughed. "But for here, for now, this'll do. Let's go see if anyone's using the bowers."

Chapter Thirty-One

They stopped at her tent to drop off their things, then Jesse followed her through the surrounding camping area to a narrow, grass covered path through the trees. They came to a three-sided shelter covering queen-size mattresses only a few feet apart. The middle one was empty, but three people occupied the right one and two the left. Lady Tina kept walking.

Another mattress filled a smaller shelter several yards away, but that also had two people on it. The path ended at a grove surrounding a stone statue of Aphrodite. Garlands of faded flowers hung around her neck, drying apples and withered grapes filled bowls at her feet, and necklaces of colored beads hung across her outstretched hand.

Lady Tina sat on the small wrought iron chair to one side of the statue and crossed one long leg over the other. Jesse dropped to his knees. She truly was worthy of a goddess' company and he wondered why she'd chosen to let him worship her.

"Isn't quite as private as the bowers," she said in a soft voice, "but it's probably one of the few places we're liable to find any privacy this time of a Sunday. We just need to keep our voices low."

Jesse didn't want to talk. He only wanted to rest his head on Lady Tina's knee and maybe, if she'd permit it, revisit the delights he'd discovered the night before.

"Now, what was your question?"

Jesse looked at her, puzzled.

"After we got your stuff out of your Sir's tent, you wanted to ask a question."

Jesse scrunched his brows together, trying to remember. "I was wondering, Ma'am, why you've taken me in." A question he should have asked Tony, apparently.

Much to his delight, Lady Tina patted her knee, and Jesse rested his cheek against her thigh with a sigh of contentment.

She ran her fingers through his still wet hair. "Because you're a sweet, confused boy who I suspect has been emotionally abused by someone in your life. Because I can help you figure who you are and where you belong. And because, I can hope that'll be at my feet wearing my collar."

Startled, Jesse lifted his head. Her smile offered hope, bliss, and passion.

"Ma'am?"

"But that's just a maybe. You've a long way to go before you can offer yourself to any woman. So let's get started."

By the time the lunch bell sounded off in the distance, Jesse had told her about the constant tension with his mother, how his father kept telling him it was okay to be gay, what hanging with the other gay guys at Skinner Butte was like. He shared his horrible first sexual experience and how discouraged he'd become when the anti-marriage equality amendment passed. She listened, stroking his hair, occasionally asking for clarification. She made no move to respond to the call for lunch and Jesse ignored the rumbling in his belly to tell her about Ashleigh and Rachel and his introduction to the joy of subspace.

"But, Ashleigh never got your consent?"

Jesse shrugged. "She and Rachel were my only friends. They accepted me. They never tried to change me."

Lady Tina sighed. "But, she handed you over to Tony without even discussing it."

Jesse wanted more than anything to chase the sad look from her eyes. "Not sure what I would have done without him, either. He got me a really awesome job where I didn't have to pretend to be something I'm not. And, he beat me almost every weekend. Mostly all I ever had to do was blow him."

"But, my dear boy, you hated that, didn't you?"

Jesse's lower lip trembled and he caught it in his teeth.

"It's okay to cry, boy. Your father may have meant well, but because he accepted society's stereotypes he set you up for years of misery and confusion." She uncrossed her legs and drew him into her arms.

He knelt between her legs, his face buried in her neck, his arms around her waist.

"Let it out, boy."

Afraid if he started crying he'd never stop, Jesse scrunched his eyes closed and bit his lip.

"Don't hold back."

He couldn't. Jesse wept. The agony of every sexual encounter before last night poured out of him. She wrapped her arms around his back and held him close. That just made him cry harder in gut wrenching sobs. He cried for every blow job he'd given, for every time he'd endured a guy fucking him in the ass, for every pretty woman's flirtation he'd ignored because he knew he was gay. He clung to Lady Tina, afraid if he released his grip, the storm of his own emotions would sweep him away.

Her arms around him brought him back to the bliss she'd shared with him last night, of the delight he found when she filled his mouth and he watched her use his cock for her pleasure. He hiccuped and tried unsuccessfully to wipe the tears from his face..

Lady Tina pressed her lips to his forehead. "Feel better?"

Surprisingly, he did. Jesse nodded.

She put her fingers under his chin and lifted his face, forcing him to look her in the eyes. "That's all in the past now. You leave it here at the feet of Aphrodite. Out there," she pointed up the path, "is your future. You ready to embrace it, whatever it brings?"

Jesse swallowed and smiled. Lady Tina reached into her pocket, pulled out a wad of tissues and handed it to him.

"Thank you, Ma'am." Jesse used most of them to clear the snot from his nose and the tears from his face. "Ma'am, what you said earlier, about me finding my place at your feet..."

She put a finger on his lips. "I find you very

attractive, boy. I like sissies. But you're not ready to get involved with anyone, just yet. Once you've got a better understanding of who you are and what you want, we can see if our needs mesh." Leaning over, she kissed him on the lips. "But we can certainly enjoy each other's company this weekend, and I'll do my best to help you figure everything out." She glanced at her watch. "Right now, though, we'd better run get lunch or we'll be stuck with leftover soup."

Jesse didn't want to leave the comfort of her embrace, but his stomach rumbled again, loudly enough for Aphrodite to hear. Reluctantly he planted a kiss on each of Lady Tina's knees and rose to his feet.

She led him back along a different path through clusters of tents brandishing Jolly Rogers and decorated with skeletons, wooden chests, and the occasional saber or cutlass. As they approached the kitchen, the tantalizing smells of spicy meat and beans assaulted his nostrils and made him salivate. When he sat down across from her with a heaping bowl of chili and a generous hunk of cornbread, he couldn't imagine anything tasting better. Except maybe the nectar he had enjoyed last night. He looked up and much to his delight, she smiled at him.

"Perhaps for dessert, boy."

Jesse's eyes widened. How the hell did she know what he was thinking?

"It's written all over your face."

He didn't care anymore how she knew the thoughts that ran through his mind. He reached across the table for her hand. She set hers on top of his, so he leaned down and kissed it, then touched his forehead to her fingers.

Chapter Thirty-Two

While Lady Tina attended a class in techniques for thoughtful tops, Jesse wandered around trying to figure out what do. The only other class on the schedule was about writing poetry and he'd no interest in that. He avoided going to the pool or hot tub, afraid if anyone tried to strike up a conversation he'd burst into tears again. He thought he saw Ashleigh and another woman checking out floggers in the vendor's area, but after his conversation with Lady Tina he wasn't sure what he would say to her so he turned away before she saw him.

At the entrance to the encampment with all the skulls and crossbones, past the sign warning "Here there be pirates," he saw Snakeman striding in his direction. Dressed all in black, he wore leather pants, knee high boots with big cuffs, a long-sleeved satin shirt with a ruffled neckline and a tri-cornered leather hat. Jolly Roger pins decorated his throat and the sides of his hat.

Jesse stepped aside to let the man pass, but Snakeman

stopped in front of him and studied him for a moment, his head cocked to one side. "What the hell did you do last night to make Tina so angry? She's not the type to kick furniture across the room."

"Nothing, Sir." Jesse looked down, unable to bear the man's penetrating stare.

"Somehow, I think there's more to it than that. What say I buy you a cup of coffee? You look like you need someone to talk to." Snakeman continued walking back toward the house.

Jesse hesitated, then scurried to catch up. It might help to talk to a complete stranger he'd never see again. Besides, he could use a decent cup of coffee. When they reached the espresso stand, Snakeman waved to the short pudgy fellow behind the counter. "I'll take my usual, Andy, and give this boy whatever he wants on my tab."

After ordering a mocha, Jesse sat across from Snakeman on the sofas at the far end of the tent.

"Nice dress." Snakeman grinned revealing jagged teeth. But his smile changed his appearance from daunting to friendly. "Convenient when you and your Mistress wear the same size."

"Lady Tina isn't my Mistress." Jesse resisted adding, *yet*.

"But, you want her to be, don't you, boy?"

Andy came over and handed them each a paper cup with a cardboard sleeve. Jesse pulled off the plastic top so he could blow on the hot coffee and avoid Snakeman's question.

Snakeman drank from his cup without waiting for it to cool."What made her so angry last night?"

Jesse savored the flavors of rich coffee and chocolate, trying to decide just how much he wanted to share. "My fucked up life."

Snakeman just stared at him.

"Specifically, my parents."

Snakeman sat his cup on the round table between them and pulled a pack of cigarettes from a leather pouch on his left hip. He offered the pack to Jesse who shook his head, then put one in his mouth and lit it. "They object to your cross dressing?"

"No, sir. They think I'm gay, but Lady Tina thinks I'm straight."

"Why does it matter what any of them think?"

Jesse shrugged his shoulders and bit his lip trying to stifle the tears that threatened to overwhelm him again.

Taking a deep drag on his cigarette, Snakeman gave Jesse the same quizzical look that had preceded his invitation to coffee. "You bisexual?"

Jesse frowned and took another sip of his coffee. He'd no idea how to answer that.

"Do you like sex with women?" Snakeman balanced his cigarette on the edge of the ashtray on the table and picked up his cup.

"I've only had sex with one woman."

Snakeman laughed. "Usually that's all it takes. Did you enjoy it?"

Jesse nodded. "Very much so."

Snakeman drank his coffee and Jesse wondered how he didn't burn his mouth. His own, open coffee still hadn't cooled past sippable, but Snakeman had never removed his lid.

"Do you like sex with men?"

Jesse slowly turned his head from left to right and back again.

"Then, I'd say you're heterosexual and it doesn't matter what either your parents or Lady Tina think."

"It's not that simple."

Snakeman removed his tri-cornered hat, set it on the sofa, and ran his hand over his bald head. "Actually, it is. Allowing other people to identify and label you just disempowers you. You're the only one who can determine your orientation, sexual or top/dominant/bottom/submissive." He picked up his cigarette and took another drag. "Many of us are flexible, depending on the relationship. I'm straight, but a femme cross dresser might catch my eye. I'm a top, but I'd consider bottoming for the right person under the right circumstances. However, these are all determinations I've made on my own. I don't let anyone else dictate my orientation, my behavior, or my moral values." He smashed the cigarette out in the pile of butts. "Why do you think it's okay to let others decide important stuff for you?"

Jesse stared at the tawny liquid in his cup, swirling it around while he contemplated Snakeman's question. He'd lived much of his life by the standards others set for him. His father had encouraged him to participate in gay youth activities and date boys. Ashleigh had seen his need for subspace, but had never asked if he wanted her to hurt him. She'd turned him over to Tony without even asking if Jesse found the man attractive. And now Lady Tina had taken him into her bed without inquiring if he wanted to be there.

He smiled. Of course, both Ashleigh and Lady Tina had given him something he liked and, indeed, now craved. He wondered if he'd have discovered how much he enjoyed either S&M or sex with women if they hadn't dragged him down that path. And, Tony *had* found him the perfect job and sent him flying. Still, if Ashleigh hadn't given him to Tony, he might have played with more women and figured out his sexuality sooner. He remembered the scene with Lady Dianne at the Sanctuary. "I guess I need to start making my own choices."

Snakeman nodded.

"But, how do I know if they're the right ones?"

"You don't." Snakeman ran his hand over his head again. "You make sure you have enough information and try to choose wisely. If you fuck it up, and you probably will at least some of the time, you apologize to anyone you hurt, pick up the pieces, and move on."

Jesse frowned. Easy for someone who was probably almost fifty to say. He felt overwhelmed and more than anything else he wanted to be back in Lady Tina's tent with his face buried in her soft breasts. He tasted the coffee again and found it cool enough to swallow. "Thanks for the coffee, Snakeman." Jesse stood.

Snakeman reached into his pouch again and extracted a business card. "Here's my contact info, kid. You can call or write if you need someone to talk to."

Jesse took the card, but didn't know where to put it. He didn't have a purse with him, and the dress had no pockets. "Thanks. I appreciate that."

Snakeman held out his right hand for Jesse to shake. "What's your name, kid?"

"Jesse, Sir."

"Okay, Jesse. Keep in touch."

Jesse smiled and left the coffee tent. He had to admit the people here at Paradise all seemed friendly, caring, and accepting. He headed back to the dining area, catching a whiff of tarragon and oregano as he passed the kitchen. He hoped that Lady Tina's class had ended.

Chapter Thirty-Three

Lady Nell let Jesse stare out the window in silence until they'd driven through the city of Tacoma, about an hour into the trip. "You gonna sulk 'til we get back to Eugene, or you gonna tell me what's going on, boy?"

Jesse shrugged.

"I know we don't know each other that well." Lady Nell's voice seemed softer, more inviting this time. "But, I'm a good confidant. Been in the lifestyle since 'fore you were born. I can just listen, or I can offer advice based on decades of experience."

Much to his surprise, Jesse burst into tears yet again. "I'm so confused."

Lady Nell patted his knee until he regained his composure. When his sobs subsided to hiccups, she asked. "Confused about what, boy?"

"I always thought I was gay. Now, it looks like I'm straight. I've no clue how to behave like a straight man."

"First of all, I very much doubt you'll ever be a

man." Lady Nell reached over and opened the glove compartment. She pulled out some Burgerville napkins and handed them to Jesse. "You're a sweet boy. You just need to behave in a way that's true to yourself. Don't worry about gay or straight."

Jesse wiped his eyes and blew his nose on the napkins, then stuffed them in his pocket. "Do *you* think I'm straight?"

"How would I know, boy? You attracted to men? You enjoy having sex with them?"

Jesse shook his head slowly from side to side. Everyone kept asking him the same question. Why hadn't anyone asked him if he found men attractive before Paradise?

Lady Nell looked to her left and pulled into the fast lane to pass a pickup hauling a horse trailer. "Not to get too personal, but how many men have you had sex with?"

Jesse had to think back. "Six."

"And you didn't enjoy it with any of them?"

Jesse hung his head.

"Why in the world did you keep having sex with guys?"

Jesse shrugged. "I wanted to have sex."

Lady Nell laughed. "Okay, I can understand that. You ever had sex with a woman, besides Lady Tina?"

Startled, Jesse turned and looked at her, wide eyed.

"I've known Lady Tina for a long time, boy. I mentored her when she first came into the scene."

"No, Ma'am, I've never had sex with a woman before this weekend."

"Because?"

Jesse scrunched his eyebrows together rather than answer.

"Don't most kids your age experiment with their sexuality? I know straight girls make out with other girls all the time."

"I wouldn't know, Ma'am. I never did." Jesse thought about how much he enjoyed watching Ashleigh and Rachel together, how lesbian porn turned him on the most when he masturbated. "I've just always known I'm gay, so I've only tried sex with men."

"But now you aren't sure?"

"Lady Tina says I'm a straight sissy boy."

"Whatever Lady Tina's opinion, you need come to terms with your own sexuality." Lady Nell glanced in the rearview mirror. "Geez, get off my tail asshole." She looked to the right and pulled back into the center lane.

"I've always assumed I was gay. Belonged to LGBT groups, haven't missed a Gay Pride festival since high school. All my friends are either gay or lesbian. Heck, even my boss is gay."

Lady Nell raised her eyebrows."And would you not work for him if you were straight?"

"I like my boss."

"Would you like him any less if you or he were straight?"

Jesse shook his head rather vigorously. "Of course not. He's a great guy. He pays well, makes his shop a fun place to work, and cares about his employees."

"Do you think being gay or not has any impact on any of that?"

He rubbed his forehead. In so many ways, Christopher fit stereotypes. He dressed, talked, and acted just like a gay hairdresser. But none of that accounted for his conscientious effort to build his business or the time he took to nurture his staff. "No."

"Did you have fun at the pride festivals?"

"Yes, Ma'am." Jesse smiled. Aside from Oregon Country Fair, pride was always his favorite summer event.

"Do you think you'd have less fun if you were straight?"

Jesse shrugged.

"See any straight people at pride?"

"A few, I guess." Jesse tried to remember who he knew at pride who wasn't gay.

"They having less fun than you?"

Jesse scratched his head. He couldn't wait to get home and take a shower in the privacy of his own bathroom.

"What makes you gay?"

"I like to wear girl's clothing, I played with dolls when I was a kid, I guess I'm effeminate." Jesse looked forward to getting out of his blue jeans and not wearing them again for a good long while.

"Does Tony wear girl's clothing, or Shane, or Demon?"

Jesse shook his head.

"Why do you think wearing girls' clothes makes you gay?"

Lady Tina's voice echoed in his head. *Because your parents accepted society's stereotypes, they set you up for years of misery and confusion.*

"What you wear, how you act, your speech -- none of that determines your sexuality." Lady Nell turned on her blinkers as they neared the Centralia exit. "You used to hang with Ashleigh and Rachel, didn't you?" She guided her Subaru station wagon, the back loaded with camping gear, off the interstate. "I need a restroom break. Could use some food, too." She turned into the Burgerville parking lot.

"You coming in, boy?"

"I guess." Jesse unbuckled his belt and stepped out of the car. He heard the click of the lock and followed Lady Nell into the restaurant.

A couple of burly men sat at the table next to the entrance, orders of onion rings in front of them and burgers in their meaty hands. One wore a Chehalis Farm Store baseball cap and a red pocket tee shirt. The other had on a Cenex shirt and a cowboy hat. They stared at Jesse when he entered.

The cowboy set his burger down on the paper wrapper. "Whatcha doin' here, faggot? We don't tolerate folks like you 'round here."

Jesse felt the heat rising to his cheeks.

"Just ignore the lummoxes." Lady Nell tugged on Jesse's arm, guiding him toward the restrooms. "They're just ignorant."

The one with the baseball cap rose to his feet."Who you callin' ignorant, bitch?"

The cowboy hat interrupted his friend, nodding his chin toward the uniformed sheriff's deputy eating lunch at the other end of the restaurant. The baseball cap sat down, but continued glowering at Jesse.

He emerged from the lavatory first, but Jesse waited by the door to the women's restroom for Lady Nell. He followed her to the counter and shook his head when she asked if he wanted anything. She ordered a burger combo meal and seemed completely at ease while she waited for it. Jesse shifted his weight from one foot to the other, wanting only to escape the restaurant and find safety in the car. When the clerk finally handed Lady Nell her bag, Jesse followed her out the door, cringing at the hateful looks thrown their way.

Chapter Thirty-Four

Lady Nell opened the wrapper on her hamburger, laying it out on her lap, before putting the car in gear and heading back to the freeway. "You can have the fries, boy. I don't need 'em and I figured you'd probably get hungry once we got away from those rednecks."

Jesse shook his head, but his stomach rumbled. He extracted the cardboard container of fries from the bag and nibbled at them. When his stomach didn't rebel, he devoured them. "Thank you, Ma'am."

Lady Nell smiled and pulled a napkin from the bag to wipe catsup from the corner of her mouth. "Now, boy, you tell me. Who're you going to believe about whether or not you're gay. Two ignoramuses at Burgerville, or a Domina who allowed you to please her sexually?"

Jesse couldn't help but laugh at that. But then he closed his eyes and leaned against the window, remembering his three exquisite nights in Lady Tina's tent. Her soft skin, her wonderful taste, the incredible feeling of her moist heat enveloping his cock. Much to his chagrin, his jeans became tight just from reminiscing. He glanced at Lady Nell, but the road and her burger kept her attention. Almost nothing Tony did made him hard, but just thinking about Lady Tina got him excited.

Lady Nell crumbled up the wrapper and put it back in the bag. "I know a lot of gay men. They're all leathermen, none effeminate." She removed the rest of the napkins from the bag and stuck them in the glove compartment. "I also know dozens of sissies. A couple of them're bisexual, but, for the most part, they're straight."

Jesse thought about Christopher and some of the members of the Imperial Court. Of course, they weren't all involved in S&M. "Is a sissy either gay or submissive?"

Lady Nell shrugged. "Straight sissies seem attracted to FemDoms, and a lot of FemDoms I know prefer sissy boys. Some even femininize boys who aren't sissies. I'm sure, if you look hard enough, you can find a straight sissy who's not involved in BDSM. But why does that matter? Only thing important here is what's right for you. You need to figure out who you are and what you want. Don't let anyone else influence you."

"Do you think I'm submissive?"

Lady Nell laughed, and laughed, and laughed, pounding the steering wheel with her fist. She ran a finger under each of eyes to wipe away the tears. "Boy, you've got to be kidding me. You served both Ashleigh and Tony. Tell me something. Did you ever attend one party at my house, at Randy's, at the Sanctuary, where some FemDom didn't hit on you?"

Jesse ran over them all in his mind. Everyone he could remember included an image of at least one woman asking him to play. He felt the heat rising to his cheeks. "It's that obvious?"

Lady Nell reached over and patted his knee. "That's not a bad thing, sweet boy."

"You said you were Lady Tina's mentor?"

"Yes."

"You know her well?"

Lady Nell shrugged. "Fairly. She moved to Seattle three years ago when she graduated. We keep in touch, but we don't see each other any more except at Paradise."

Jesse added the empty french fry box to the bag. "Would you know what she might expect from her submissive?"

"Same thing we all want, boy." Lady Nell sipped at her soda. "Love, devotion, loyalty. Someone who enjoys serving his Domme for the pleasure it gives her, not for what he can get out of it. However, if someone accepts ownership, they also accept a lot responsibility." She glanced at Jesse for a moment before turning her eyes back to the road. "And you shouldn't offer yourself to anyone who hasn't earned your love, respect, and trust. Does Tony have any of those?"

"Well, I guess I trust him. And I respect him. He's always been straight with me." Jesse sniggered at his unintended joke. "I mean, he never lied to me or anything."

"But did he earn your trust or did you just hand it over to him because Ashleigh told you to?"

Jesse frowned. How did someone earn your trust? "I wouldn't have my job at Wild Roots if it weren't for Tony and I really like working there."

"Did Tony ever do anything that you hadn't agreed

to. Or that you asked him not to do?"

Jesse shrugged. He'd never really agreed to allow Tony to do anything. "I didn't really have much to say about it."

Lady Nell looked at him again, only this time she stared long enough for the car to drift across the white line. Someone behind them honked, making them both jump. She regained control, and kept her eyes on the road. "Are you telling me that Tony never asked you to submit to him?"

"Ashleigh never asked, either. She just told me what to do and I did it. Can't really blame Tony, though. Apparently Ashleigh gave me to him."

"Without your consent? Why, boy, why? Do you have no sense of self respect?"

"Isn't that kind of necessary to be submissive?"

"Absolutely not. That's what most folks call a doormat. And you wipe your feet on a doormat. You don't invite it into your home, your heart, and your bed." Lady Nell picked up her cup and sucked on the soda until it produced slurping sounds from the bottom. "You need to learn to stand up for yourself, boy. Unless you've given someone permission to put a collar around your neck, you've absolutely no obligation to obey that person."

Jesse pulled his knees up to his chest and kept his face buried against his legs through Vancouver and Portland. When Lady Nell again pulled off the freeway for a bathroom break, no one at this Burgerville spoke to them except for the clerk who took Jesse's order for a hamburger and shake and Lady Nell's for another soda.

After Lady Nell maneuvered the car back onto the freeway, she asked him, "Have you ever taken any classes or gone to the Wednesday night open house at Randy's?"

Jesse shook his head and took a sip of his shake.

Lady Nell sighed. "With all the resources available in Eugene, why didn't you take advantage of some of them?"

Jesse swallowed the last bit of his hamburger and crumpled the paper. "I don't know that I've ever thought about it. I just like to fly on endorphins. Until this weekend, I preferred it to sex. Now, I'm not so sure."

Lady Nell laughed and reached over to pat him on the knee again. "Sweetie, we're wired differently. We need the combination of flying and sex. One without the other just doesn't cut it."

"But Lady Tina plays with girls even though she's straight."

"Playing with someone you don't want to have sex with, still gets you charged up. It makes the sex you do have better."

Jesse closed his eyes. He had so much to think about, so much to learn. "Lady Tina'd want someone who'd serve as her submissive, not just someone she could play with and enjoy sexually?"

"Of course."

"How do I learn, how do I figure out, what do I need to do to ..." Jesse knew he still had a lot of issues to work out. He had some serious thinking to do. But, one thing he knew for sure already: when all was said and done, he wanted more than anything to earn his place at Lady Tina's feet, wearing her collar.

"Well, for starters, come to the open house tomorrow. I'll introduce you to some of the younger folk. Madame

Sabrina leads discussion groups and training sessions on the weekends. While you're there, you can ask Randy to add you to the listserv so you get notices of classes and workshops."

Jesse took a deep breath. If he wasn't spending his weekends with Tony, he certainly would have time on his hands. He also had Lady Tina's e-mail address and telephone number. Perhaps she could suggest some areas for him to study, ways he could learn to please her. "Thanks, Lady Nell. I really appreciate the ride home and your willingness to let me vent." He took a slug from his milkshake and let the cold slide down his throat. "Do you think Lady Tina might accept me as her submissive if I study hard and learn how to serve her."

Lady Nell smiled. "She'd be crazy not to." Jesse relaxed a little. "You're a sweet, pretty boy with a high pain tolerance. I imagine she'd be delighted to consider you."

Jesse smiled, too.

Epilogue

Jesse paced back and forth across his small apartment. He'd changed his clothes five times, from skirt to jeans to dress to slacks and finally to a simple straight skirt and silky royal blue blouse. His meager belongings, mostly clothing and accessories, filled only three boxes. He'd take them with on the train him in the morning. He'd given the few pieces of furniture he had to the couple taking over his lease.

During the past week, he'd said goodbye to everyone at the open house and the regular parties. Christopher had written him a wonderful letter of recommendation that made it easy for him to find a position at a premier Seattle salon. Only one more piece in the puzzle of his life in Eugene needed putting away before he could leave for his new life in Seattle. He fiddled with the bow on the wrapped package sitting on top of one of the boxes.

He jumped when he heard a knock on the door. He took a deep breath and opened it.

"Hello, son." His dad stepped in and looked around.

"You moving?"

"Please, have a seat." Jesse pointed to the futon sofa. "Can I get you anything to drink?"

"Sure. You have coffee?"

Jesse frowned. "Sorry, I already packed the coffee maker. Mountain Dew, bottled water, or Arizona Tea?"

"Tea's fine. Thanks." His dad accepted the proffered bottle, settled on the couch, opened the cap and took a swig.

Jesse sat on the edge of the kitchen chair that he'd placed in front of the sofa. "I'm moving to Seattle to be with someone."

His dad smiled. "You've met a fella. That's great news, son. How'd you meet him? How long've you known him? Will you go to Canada and get married, or are you just going to do a civil union thing?"

"I met her at an event I attended in Washington last summer."

His dad's face turned red, then white and his eyes opened wider than Jesse thought possible. "Her?"

"Yes ... her. Over the past year, I've come to realize I'm not gay, I'm straight. I just like wearing women's clothing and I prefer to adopt a more feminine persona."

His dad sat with his mouth working, but nothing came out for what felt like several minutes. Finally, he said: "Oh ... my ... fucking ... God." He put his hands on his head and closed his eyes. "What the hell ...?"

"It's okay, Dad." Ironically, Jesse found himself wanting to comfort his father. "I've learned a lot about myself in the past year. Reality is that there're things that've become important in my life. Good things that I might not've discovered if I'd lived in the straight community."

Jesse picked up the wrapped package and held it in his lap. "Although I'm heterosexual, I'm not exactly what folks in this society consider normal. For one, in addition to being a sissy, I'm a submissive and a masochist." Jesse found freedom in using those words to identify himself. They described who he was in terms others understood, even if his parents never would. "The woman I'm going to Seattle to be with is Lady Tina. She's a FemDom and I hope to become her collared slave."

His dad took a gulp from his tea bottle and choked. After coughing for long enough that Jesse started to worry, his dad took a deep breath. "I don't understand," he gasped, then coughed some more. "Why'd you want to be someone's slave? What exactly are you talking about?"

Jesse handed him the package. "This'll help you understand some things about alternative sexuality and lifestyles."

His dad stared at the package, but made no move to unwrap it.

"It's a book called *When Someone You Love Is Kinky*. If you read it, you'll a little bit about how and why I'm different."

His dad looked up, still pale, sweat beading up on his forehead.

"The important thing for you to know is that I've found someone I adore and who I want to spend the rest of my life with. She loves me just the way I am." He picked up his skirt and fingered the silky material. "In fact, she likes me to wear women's clothing."

"So, will you get married? Have kids?" His dad gripped the book as if it was some kind of life ring. "I mean, will you live a normal life?"

"I don't think you could really call anything about our life normal." He touched the gold chain around his neck, Lady Tina's collar of consideration. A tiny padlock held the two ends together. She'd promised him that when she put her permanent collar on him, he'd not be able to remove it without bolt cutters. "But, we may choose to get married for the legal benefits. Lady Tina has said she might want to have children someday. Hopefully, she'll find me worthy of fathering them."

His father took a long slow swallow from the bottle. "What the hell am I going to tell your mother?"

Jesse sighed. "Honestly, I don't care. She never accepted me in any way. Not really. I think she fought so hard against Measure 36 because if I married some guy at least that would make me seem more normal. Well, I'm not normal. I'll never be normal, and I really don't want to be normal. I've found a community where I'm accepted and appreciated and a woman who loves me exactly the way I am. My mother never did."

To his surprise, a tear trickled down his dad's cheek. "She does love you son. In her own way." His dad swiped at his cheek with the back of his hand. "She's not very good at showing it, but she only wants you to be happy." He picked up the book. "I'll read this and decide if she can handle it."

His dad's shoulders shook and for a moment he held one hand over his face. "I'm so sorry son." He made a strange sound in his throat, almost like a frog croaking. "We just assumed ... you liked so many girlie things. You know, your mother kept all your Barbie dolls. They're still in the attic."

"I'll admit that dating guys resulted in some pretty awful things ... but no permanent damage. I've learned a lot about myself, and I don't think I'd have found my Lady if ..." Would he have gone to Paradise if Tony hadn't taken him? Would Ashleigh have introduced him to S&M if she'd thought he was straight?

Jesse went to the fridge and got himself a can of Mountain Dew. He opened it and swallowed about half. Even if he'd discovered BDSM as a straight, he thought about all the FemDoms who'd flirted with him. He'd found some of them quite attractive. If he'd gotten involved with one, he might never have met Lady Tina. And although he'd hated sex with Tony, the man had introduced Jesse to CBT which allowed him to demo bottom for Lady Tina.

He cleared his throat. "I may or may not have gotten to this point in my life if I hadn't been raised thinking I was gay. But, let's face it, the world's just as harsh for sissy guys as it is for gays and lesbians. Perhaps more so."

"This Lady, she loves you? She makes you happy?"

"She's my Goddess. I'd do anything for her and serving her's my greatest pleasure."

His dad frowned. "Does she take advantage of you?"

"A Mistress/slave relationship's symbiotic, not parasitic. Lady Tina's a very responsible FemDom and she does love me. It may not be the same kind of love you share with mother, but it's profound and intense."

For the first time since he sat down on the futon, the crease between his dad's eyebrows disappeared. "I hope you'll invite us to the wedding."

"To be honest, I'm not sure there'll be a traditional

wedding. Lady Tina's planning a ceremony when I've earned her collar, though. I can let you know when that'll be, and you can decide if you want to attend. And whether or not you want to bring Mom."

"I assume you'll explain to me what kind of ceremony it is before I try to decide whether or not to bring her along. But I want to be there, even if I don't have a clue. I love you son. I've always loved you. I just want you to be happy."

His dad dug into the pocket of his jeans, extracted a handkerchief and blew his nose. "I'm so sorry I made assumptions instead of letting you grow up and figure things out for yourself. I hope you can forgive me."

Jesse stood up and opened his arms. His dad jumped to his feet and wrapped his arms around him. They stood that way for almost ten minutes, just holding each other, his dad occasionally sniffling.

His dad finally released him and stepped back. "I take it from the state of things, you're leaving soon?"

"I'm taking the nine o'clock train tomorrow morning."

His dad looked around. "The boxes going with?"

Jesse nodded.

"How 'bout I pick you up at eight so we have plenty of time to get you over there and get everything checked in."

Jesse smiled. "Thanks, Dad."

◇◇◇◇◇◇◇◇
Acknowledgements

This book would not have reached your hands without the help of many dear friends and colleagues. I thank my readers and supporters, especially: Cindy, my proofreader, editor and best friend; Deborah Dixon and Lane Alexandra, first readers; my hairdresser, Julie; Snakeman who dontated a large sum to RCDC for the honor of appearing on these pages and whose character then became pivotal to Jesse's transformation; and the wonderful volunteers and staff at Paradise. Thanks especially to my beloved submissive, Patrick for his love, his support, and his service.

Other novels by Korin I. Dushayl include:

Broken
Some things can never be fixed

Given a choice between slavery and ostracization, Jessica chooses to kneel naked before her department head so she can continue studying for her PhD in psychology. That decision takes her down a dark path to abuse, exploitation, and torment of both her body and her spirit.

Korin I. Dushayl "writes with authority and compassion about those who live within the lifestyle. Broken and Shattered explore issues including finding and initiating a submissive partner, informed consent, and the difference between dominating someone and exploiting their needs."

Elizabeth Coldwell
author, anthologist, magazine editor

Buy it in Print

or E-Book

Shattered
Just where do you cross the point of no return?

When a sweet, intelligent twenty-five year old with undiagnosed Asperser and PTSD seeks help from a ruthless, unscrupulous, sadistic therapist, she shatters his psyche and throws him into a suicidal depression. Her crude attempt to pick up the pieces -- enslaving him and subjecting him to unethical, unsanctioned, experiments -- ignores the lines of consent and the responsibilities of a Dominant. -- Inspired by a true story.

"The work ... unfolds with the assured touch of a best-selling mainstream author, seducing us into the lives of people with needs and agendas that find wings in the dark. Only an author familiar with this landscape could peel back these layers of psychological complexity without flinching and without dramatic compromise ... Prepare to submit to this reading experience, which will mark you with its narrative power.

Larry Brooks, USA Today bestselling author of
Darkness Bound and *Bait and Switch*

Buy it in Print

or E-Book

Choices

Must Linda's sexual awakening destroy her marriage?

From fairy tales to modern legal tradition, society demands we love exclusively, even though many only find happiness with multiple partners. Linda finally confronts long neglected sexual needs when Phil forces himself on her in Chicago. But back in Portland, her husband's insistence on monogamy compels her to choose between his limitations and her own insatiable desires.

Buy it in Print

or E-Book

For more information visit
http://transgressivewriter.com